THE AVENGERS

The criminal mastermind known only as 'Simon Boyle' has amassed a vast fortune defrauding banks. Scotland Yard, unable to identify and apprehend him, is forced to call in private detective John Blackmore. Blackmore's investigations lead to Boyle's arrest — but not before he brutally murders the detective's informant. After his trial, still hiding his real identity, Boyle faces execution. But his vow, that he will be avenged, threatens that Blackmore and those responsible for his death will be killed . . .

DERWENT STEELE

THE AVENGERS

Complete and Unabridged

LINFORD
Leicester

First published in Great Britain

First Linford Edition
published 2011

British Library CIP Data

Steele, Derwent.
   The avengers. - - (Linford mystery library)
   1. Private investigators- -Great Britain- -
   Fiction. 2. Fraud- -Fiction. 3. Informers- -
   Crimes against- -Fiction. 4. Detective and
   mystery stories. 5. Large type books.
   I. Title II. Series
   823.9'12–dc22

   ISBN 978–1–44480–647–2

Published by
F. A. Thorpe (Publishing)
Anstey, Leicestershire

Set by Words & Graphics Ltd.
Anstey, Leicestershire
Printed and bound in Great Britain by
T. J. International Ltd., Padstow, Cornwall

This book is printed on acid-free paper

1

The man who was going to tell

John Blackmore came out of the Whitehall entrance to Scotland Yard, and ignoring the enquiring gaze of a dawdling taxi driver began to walk slowly in the direction of Trafalgar Square.

There was a frown between the detective's level brows, for his interview with the Chief Commissioner and Detective-Inspector Kenton had given him much food for thought. The subject of that interview concerned one Simon Boyle, who, for ten years had been engaged in the systematic forging and uttering of letters of credit, bills of exchange and other negotiable securities.

Actually there was no such person as Simon Boyle. It was merely a label that indicated his activities and had been the name on the cheque presented by a bluff, stout, hearty man, at the West Wicham branch of the Surrey Bank ten years previously and which had cost that establishment exactly seven thousand pounds. It was the first name by which he was known and served to mark him on the record cards at Scotland Yard.

The military looking man, who, six months later got sixteen thousand pounds out of the Bank of Exchange by means of a forged warrant, was, undoubtedly, the same person, with a moustache and horn-rimmed glasses. The Bank manager who coolly walked out of the Bank of England with thirty thousand pounds which he took on behalf of the Capital and Counties had no moustache and was minus the glasses, but it was certain that he and Simon Boyle went about in their leisure moments under the same hat.

These were but a few of the man's audacious and daring coups, and so clever was he and possessed such genius with his pen that only on one occasion during the many years in which he had followed his nefarious business had he personally come in contact with the police. A certain Inspector Parsons who had been given the job of running this master forger to earth succeeded by some means in getting on his track.

He was a reticent man, and liked to place before his superiors the finished result of his work rather than supply them with the daily details of his investigations. And this proved his undoing, for he was found with six inches of steel in his back at the side of a lonely road between Putney and Wimbledon Common. He had been dead some hours, for Mr. Simon Boyle supported the cleverness of his pen with violence.

The Banking world was in something like a panic, for this clever and elusive man had bled them all indiscriminately and for large sums. Their attitude to the police was, in consequence, both bitter and acrimonious, and in desperation the Chief Commissioner had sent for John Blackmore.

'We can't catch him because we don't know him,' said that gloomy and depressed official at the interview. 'But mostly because he works alone. If there was a woman attached to him, or if he ran a gang or had a partner of any kind he wouldn't have lasted a year. He's clever enough to work on his own and there's nobody to give him away.'

John Blackmore had agreed with these words of wisdom, and had accepted the suggestion that he should go out after Mr. Simon Boyle.

'No, I don't want to see the records,' he replied, in answer to Kenton's offer to supply him with everything that was known regarding Boyle. 'I've got a detailed account of all his exploits among my own cuttings. I only want one thing, and that is, a completely free hand. On that condition I'll do my best.'

The condition was readily granted, and a little later Blackmore had left the Yard to walk back to Mecklinburg Square and immerse himself in all that was known about the career of Mr. Simon Boyle. He elected to walk because he had a lot to think about and the gentle exercise stimulated his brain.

The task he had undertaken was no light one. In spite of various novelists' repeated assertions to the contrary the police are by no means the bunch of thick-headed numbskulls they are made out to be, and nobody knew this better than John Blackmore. The Criminal Investigation Branch of the Metropolitan Police Force contains some of the shrewdest brains in the world, but their methods are conventional and hampered by tradition and red tape. Therefore, if they, in ten years, had failed to catch Simon Boyle he would require a lot of catching.

Still thinking the matter over in his mind John Blackmore was suddenly roused from his thoughts by a light touch on his arm, and looking round saw a small, shabby, furtive-eyed man shuffling along by his side.

'Hullo, Henry,' he said in surprise. 'I thought you were in prison.'

'Came out last week,' said 'Harry the Dip,' and then urgently: 'When can I 'ave a talk to you, Mr. Blackmore?'

'What's the matter with now?' answered the detective, but the little man shook his head and then glanced quickly about him.

'No, I might be spotted,' he said. 'I'm takin' a chance as it is speakin' ter yer at all.' His snubbed nose wrinkled in thought. 'I got a room in Greek Street,' he went on, 'could yer come along there — to-night — about 'leven?'

John Blackmore looked down at him curiously.

'What's the idea, Harry?' he asked. 'What do you want to see me about?'

'I can't tell yer 'ere,' the man looked up and down the crowded street again nervously, and there was a quiver of fear in his voice. 'I believe I'm bein' trailed.'

'Trailed — by the police, do you mean?' said Blackmore, and Harry shook his head impatiently.

'Perlice! No, that wouldn't worry me,' he said contemptuously. 'No, it's a feller what came to see me last night. Wanted me to do a job fer 'im.' He broke off. 'I'll tell yer all about it when yer come to-night. My address is 102 — top floor. You heard of Simon Boyle ain't yer. Well, it's about 'im.'

He turned suddenly and went shuffling away in the opposite direction, leaving Blackmore with his mind in a whirl.

It was an extraordinary coincidence.

Less than an hour after he had been asked to try and find that elusive gentleman here was a clue more or less dropped from the clouds. If it should lead anywhere it was a sheer piece of luck. He continued his walk thoughtfully.

What did 'Harry the Dip' know? It was an open secret that the little crook occupied his time between his lapses from honesty in a little judicious 'nosing,' and the Bankers' Association had offered a reward of a thousand pounds to anybody who could give information that would lead to the capture of Simon Boyle. But what had he found out about the forger? Evidently something in connection with the job he had been asked to do on the previous night.

John Blackmore let himself into his house with a feeling of intense curiosity, and this feeling remained with him throughout the remainder of the afternoon and evening, despite the fact that he set himself to work and read through the mass of information contained in the cuttings devoted to the doings of Simon Boyle.

It was almost on the stroke of eleven

when he reached Greek Street. Number 102 proved to be a dingy building, the entrance to which was between two eating houses and consisted of a narrow door badly in need of a fresh coat of paint and boasting a rusty iron knocker. The detective raised his hand and rapped sharply. He had to repeat the summons twice before he heard a shuffling footfall and then the door was opened by a slatternly woman who peered at him suspiciously.

'What d'you want?' she growled, and the detective explained.

'Oh, yes. He said he was expectin' a gentleman. Will you go straight up. His room is the second door on the top landing.'

Blackmore thanked her and made his way up the dark and evil smelling staircase. There was no light and he had to feel his way by the banister. He reached the top landing and in the faint glow from a nearby electric sign that filtered through a dirty window saw two doors, one near the head of the staircase and one directly facing him. From underneath this latter came a thin pencil of light, and concluding that this was the abode of the man he was seeking the detective crossed the intervening patch of bare boards and tapped.

No answering voice bade him enter, and thinking that perhaps Harry had dropped into a doze he rapped again, louder. Still there was silence and impatiently he gripped the handle and turned it. The door was unlocked, and pushing it open he entered.

'I've come along as you asked me, Harry,' he said, pausing on the threshold and addressing the little crook who was lying back in a moth-eaten armchair by the table. 'Wake up!'

'Harry the Dip' took no notice, and stepping over Blackmore shook him gently by the shoulder. The man in the chair slumped sideways and then rolled on to the floor — to lie motionless, a sprawling, horrible, ungainly figure.

With a sharp exclamation Blackmore looked at his fingers. They were shiny and red! The next second he saw the cause. 'Harry the Dip' was dead! Had been killed with the knife that remained buried in his chest!

2

The Message in Blood

For perhaps a minute John Blackmore stood looking down at the motionless figure of the little crook, his lips set in a tight thin line. Then, wiping the blood from his fingers with his handkerchief he went to the door, and making his way to the head of the staircase called the woman who had let him in. She came, after a long delay, with much laboured breathing and a demand to know what it was he wanted.

'Go and fetch the nearest policeman,' he ordered sharply. 'There's been a serious crime committed here to-night.'

She stared at him with dropped jaw and then began a flood of questions but Blackmore cut them short.

'Go and do as I tell you,' he said. 'And ask the constable to 'phone to his station for the ambulance and the Divisional Surgeon.'

'What is it, Mister?' asked the woman, her eyes bulging in terror. 'What's happened?'

The detective saw that the quickest way to get rid of her was to tell her the truth, so he briefly explained.

It had the desired effect. She hurried away, muttering lamentations concerning the reputation of the establishment, and he went back to the room of death.

The place that had been 'Harry the Dip's' home was small and poorly furnished, little more than an attic. A washstand behind the door, a broken bed, a plain-topped deal table, and the dilapidated arm-chair in which the dead man had been seated were the only items of furniture. An oil lamp provided a dim light, and standing just inside the doorway Blackmore allowed his eyes to rove about the miserable apartment.

So far as he could see there were no signs of a struggle — death had come swiftly and unexpectedly. There was a half finished glass of beer on the table, flanked by an empty bottle and a plate on which were the remains of some bread and

11

cheese. 'Harry the Dip' had apparently been eating his supper when the fatal blow had been struck that had robbed him of his life. But how had the killer got in without rousing the little crook's suspicions? The obvious answer was that he had been somebody sufficiently well known and friendly with Harry to have come in without causing him any uneasiness.

John Blackmore frowned. This seemed to eliminate Simon Boyle, and yet he was convinced that the unknown forger was responsible for the murder. The coincidence was too great to believe otherwise. 'Harry the Dip' had asked Blackmore to come and see him — had more than hinted that he had something to tell the detective about Boyle, and Blackmore had arrived to find a knife in his chest and his lips sealed for ever. He remembered his evident fear of the morning and his assertion that he was being trailed. Had Boyle witnessed the interview in the street — been sufficiently close to have overheard the time and place of the appointment and laid his plans accordingly? That he was a killer when his own safety was at stake had been proved by the cold-blooded way in which he had disposed of Parsons. But how had he managed the deed? All the data collected by the police went to show that he played a lone hand, and yet 'Harry the Dip' would never have remained quietly seated in his chair while the man he was about to betray entered the room.

Blackmore himself had been a witness of the informer's fear. Harry would have put up some sort of a fight unless his visitor was one with whom he felt perfectly safe. He had mentioned something about a man who had asked him to do a job — was this man Boyle?

The detective gave a slight shrug to his shoulders. It was useless speculating. Whatever Harry had been going to tell him was now lost for ever. There was, however, the chance that his murderer had left behind some form of clue, and in this hope Blackmore began a search of the room.

He found nothing until he came upon a crumpled evening paper that lay inside the armchair, and he was tossing this aside when he saw that it was smeared with several red lines and blotches. With a little thrill of excitement he spread the paper out on the table and studied it under the oil lamp.

The wavering lines had been traced across the paper by a finger dipped in blood! And with much difficulty the detective succeeded in deciphering the message.

'Boyle ... 24 ... Uni ... Ba ... Colchest ... '

The 'T' trailed away into a meaningless smear.

In his death agony Harry had tried to deliver his message, and had died before it was completed. Blackmore could make no sense out of the almost illegible scrawl, but he tore the strip from the paper and folding it, stowed it away in his pocket. A heavy step on the stair heralded the arrival of the policeman.

He evidently knew 'Harry the Dip' for he shook his head when he learned of the terrible crime.

'Poor Harry,' he commented. 'Been 'nosing' on someone and they or them done 'im in. I 'phoned the inspector, Mr. Blackmore, and 'e's comin' round with the ambulance. I'll just take down the details. I suppose you don't know who it was who killed 'im?'

John Blackmore shook his head. He made no mention of Boyle or of the last message the dead man had tried to leave.

The constable began writing laboriously in his note book, and was still so engaged when the inspector arrived, and with him the divisional surgeon.

'As far as I can tell from a superficial examination,' said the doctor, after he had inspected the body, 'he's been dead for about an hour. The blow was obviously struck from behind, and from the expression on his face I should say he was taken by surprise. He didn't die instantly. I should say that he must have lingered for five or six minutes, perhaps longer.'

Inquiries of the woman who owned the house were unsatisfactory. No visitors, with the exception of Blackmore, had been to see the dead man, of that she was certain. He had come in about nine o'clock and told her he had been to the pictures. She had brought up his supper at nine thirty, which had consisted of a bottle of beer and some bread and cheese and he had then informed her that he was expecting a gentleman to call at eleven, and asked her to send him straight up. She thought he had appeared rather more excited than usual and had spoken about shortly having a lot of money, but she had taken very little notice of this. 'Harry the Dip' had occupied his room here for some years and was given to exaggeration.

Blackmore and the inspector made a thorough examination of the room. There was a hanging curtain across one corner, with hooks driven into the wall for clothes and on the floor of this recess they found fresh traces of muddy foot-prints.

'That's where the murderer concealed himself,' said the detective. 'He was probably hiding behind this curtain when the woman brought up Harry's supper.'

'It looks like it,' answered the inspector. 'But how the deuce did he get in?'

'So far as I can see,' said Blackmore, 'there's only one possible way, and that's through the window on the landing.' He led the way out into the landing and examined the window. 'This has been opened recently. Look!' He pointed to where the grime of ages had been disturbed between the frame and the moulding.

The inspector pushed the window up and looked out. At one time or other an outside service for the use of tradesmen had been built and the iron framework ran up close beside the window.

'That's the way he came and that's the way he went,' said the inspector.

John Blackmore looked down into a square courtyard below. The window was roughly sixty feet from the ground but it would have been possible for an active man to have climbed the framework of the service lift and to have swung himself from there to the sill.

'Yes, I think you're right,' said the detective, and withdrew his head.

The ambulance removed the remains of 'Harry the Dip' and shortly afterwards John Blackmore went home. It was nearly two when he reached Mecklinburg

Square and found that his secretary had gone to bed. Slipping into his dressing gown he lit a cigarette and switching on the light on his desk he sat down with the bloodstained newspaper spread out before him.

Dawn was breaking when he rose and took a book down from one of the well-filled shelves. Turning the pages rapidly he found what he sought, and when he returned it to its place his eyes were shining.

'I think that will settle you, Mr. Simon Boyle,' he muttered, as he made his way to his bedroom to snatch a few hours' sleep.

He had solved the riddle of 'Harry the Dip's' last message, and thought he saw the end of the elusive forger and killer in sight. In one way he was right, except that the end in this case, was to be but the beginning.

3

The Threat

One fine spring morning — it was the 24th of April to be exact — and a week after the inquest had been held on 'Harry the Dip' — Mr. Simon Boyle drove through the dingy little town of Chelmsford on his way to Colchester. He passed a high wall of red brick and a grim black gateway and smiled, for prison had no terrors for Mr. Boyle. He had colossal faith in his own ability and organising power and considered himself immune from the pitfalls that surrounded the feet of lesser criminals.

The law, with its swift penalties for the wrong-doer was a thing — if not to be treated lightly — at least to be regarded in its proper place. Little sneak thieves and smash-and-grab men rightly feared its long arm, but not such artists as Mr. Simon Boyle. He stroked the moustache he had so carefully cultivated for the past three months and hummed a gay little tune as he drove along.

Just outside Colchester he turned his car into a side lane, took from beneath the seat a small suit case that contained a razor and a change of clothing that would, in the shortest possible time change his appearance into a rather seedy looking parson, walked jauntily to the place where the tram-cars start, boarded one, and was jerked and jolted uncomfortably to the centre of the town.

It was a little after eleven when he entered the door of the United Bank and wished a cheery good morning to the cashier, and laid down a paper and a book.

The cashier examined both carefully while Mr. Boyle smoothed his moustache and tapped impatiently on the counter.

'How will you have this, Colonel Rossiter?' he enquired.

'In tens,' said Mr. Boyle with a rather bored air.

The cashier produced pads of notes and he counted them rapidly, writing the numbers in his book.

'Thank you,' he said at length, pushing two large wads towards the military looking man, and Mr. Boyle picked them up and placed them carefully in his pocket.

'Good morning,' he said, politely, and turned.

There had only been two people in the bank when he had entered, a girl, tall and rather pretty, and an exquisitely dressed young man with a monocle who was talking to a clerk, but now the doorway seemed to be full of people — big men, with the unmistakable stamp of Scotland Yard.

'I want you, Simon Boyle!'

A clear decisive voice cut into the silence, and a tall, lean man detached himself from the group in the doorway and advanced.

John Blackmore! Boyle stopped, his face a shade paler, his hands clenched.

'Are you talking to me?' he said, pulling himself together with an effort. 'I'm afraid you've made a mistake.'

'I don't think so,' answered the

detective, grimly, and at that moment Simon Boyle flew at him.

In a second the centre of the floor was a struggling heap of men — a whirlpool of thrashing arms and legs and straining bodies.

The immaculate youth who had been talking to the clerk joined in and then Boyle tore himself free of the mêlée and leaped to his feet, an automatic gripped in his hands!

The girl screamed a second before the deafening explosion of the shot rang out and one of the plain clothes men went down, his face streaming with blood. The man who had been behind him pluckily tried to grasp the forger's pistol wrist, but Boyle fired again and the bullet shattered the detective's arm.

Panting, with his lips curled in a snarl of defiance, Simon Boyle sprang for the door, but he never reached it. A vice-like grip fastened on his ankle and he was jerked violently off his feet. He fell with a crash that all but knocked the breath out of him and his pistol went flying from his hand.

'Put the irons on him,' ordered John Blackmore, rising to his feet, 'and get somebody to phone the nearest hospital.' He looked down at the limp heap of the Scotland Yard man and the ever increasing pool of blood. 'You'll pay for that, Boyle. I thought you never carried a gun?'

Simon Boyle said nothing, but he glared murder at his captor as Inspector Kenton snapped the handcuffs on his wrists.

★ ★ ★

The trial which followed in due course was one of the most sensational that had filled the Central Criminal Court at the Old Bailey for many a long day. Thousands of people were turned away and on the day that it ended and sentence was passed on Simon Boyle, newspapers were at a premium, and as much as half a crown was paid for a copy containing the verdict!

There had been no hope for Boyle from the first. His counsel had done his best, and if it hadn't been for the deliberate murder of the plain clothes man at the bank he might have got off. The capital charge for the killing of 'Harry the Dip' and Parsons would have been difficult to bring home to him for there was no direct evidence.

Throughout his trial Boyle remained silent, a stolid figure, carefully groomed, who stood in the dock looking straight before him and apparently taking no interest whatever in the proceedings. He shook his head when Mr. Edward Mallin asked him if he had anything to say, and heard the death sentence without outwardly turning a hair.

The name Simon Boyle, which nobody believed to be his own stuck to him because he steadfastly refused to give any other or offer any information concerning himself whatever.

After the trial was over he was removed to Chelmsford Jail to await his execution, and two days before the date fixed for this John Blackmore received a message from the Governor saying that Boyle had expressed a desire to see him. The morning before he paid the penalty for his crimes, much against his will, the detective acceded to the request and arrived before the gates of the prison as the clock was striking seven. He rang the bell, and the warder who answered took him through a little lobby and along a narrow passage to the Governor's office.

The Governor was alone, for the other officials peculiar to such an occasion had not yet arrived.

'The Chaplain is with him now,' said the Governor. 'I hope it isn't going to be very painful for you Mr. Blackmore, but he was very insistent.'

John Blackmore nodded.

'Why does he want to see me?' he asked.

'I don't know.' The Governor shook his head. 'But the last question he put to me last night was whether you would be coming.'

He rose and led the way along a stone corridor at the end of which was a heavy steel door. A warder was stationed outside and at a sign from his superior he unlocked the door.

'Wait a moment,' said the Governor,

and went in to the cell.

A moment later he came out and beckoned Blackmore, and with a heavy sensation at his heart the detective entered the chamber of death.

Simon Boyle was seated on the plank bed. He was collarless, that item of his wardrobe had been removed that morning, and a stubble of beard covered his chin. A cigarette hung limply from his lower lip.

'Sit down Blackmore,' he made room at his side, but the detective declined. He preferred to stand. 'I thought I'd like to see you before I went out.' Boyle removed the cigarette and twisted it about in his fingers — long slim, artist's fingers Blackmore noted mechanically. 'I've committed three murders in my time and now you think I'm going to pay, don't you? You're wrong! They'll hang me and bury me but I shall still live! And I'll get you, Mr. John Blackmore! I'll get every man who brought me to my death!'

'You're crazy, Boyle!' broke in the white faced Governor. 'If I'd known — '

'What I was going to say, you wouldn't

have persuaded Blackmore to come and see me,' finished Simon Boyle coldly. 'I guessed that. Well, think I'm crazy if you like, but remember what I've said. My vengeance shall extend beyond the grave. My dead hand strike at all those who have been my enemies!' There was a curious light in his eyes. 'You can go now,' he said curtly. 'That's all I've got to say to you!'

'What do you think he meant?' asked the Governor. 'Good Heavens! the man must be mad!'

John Blackmore said nothing, he was busy thinking.

He didn't wait and he was passing through a little village on his way back when he heard a clock strike eight. Stopping the car he removed his hat, for at that moment he knew that Simon Boyle's soul had passed to eternity.

The last stroke faded away and then — Crash!

The windscreen shivered to fragments in front of him, and the second bullet drilled a neat round hole in the hat he still held in his hand!

4

The Unknown Hand

During the month that followed three attempts were made on John Blackmore's life. After he had been fired at on his journey back after his interview with Simon Boyle, he searched the countryside without finding any trace of the concealed shooter. Continuing on his way to London he had garaged his car, and was in the act of inserting the key in his front door of the house in Mecklinburg Square when a knife had skimmed past his ear, and stuck quivering in the panel in front of him.

There was a stream of traffic passing and it could have come from any one of the closed cars and taxi-cabs that were going by. He kept the knife as a souvenir, but after that he was very watchful.

His watchfulness, however, didn't save him from a narrow escape three nights later. He had been to a theatre with Cartwright, and the weather being fine they decided to walk home. In Holborn, a car driven at furious speed suddenly twisted from its course and mounted the sidewalk. The radiator was within a foot of Blackmore's back when Cartwright dragged him clear in the nick of time. Several people saw the incident, but the car had righted itself and swung down a side turning before they fully realised what had happened, and nobody could remember the number.

'It's sheer coincidence,' grunted Inspector Kenton, when he heard it. 'Can't be anything else. Simon Boyle's dead and buried, and he didn't work with a gang or a partner. Thousands of people have got grudges against you, Blackmore. It must be somebody else.'

John Blackmore shrugged his shoulders, but he didn't argue, and Kenton changed his opinion on his own accord when, a week later, a patrolling policeman found the dead body of Mr. James Lane, K.C., lying by the side of the road in a quiet street off Bloomsbury Square. He had been stabbed in the back and was stone dead!

'Lane was the counsel for the prosecution,' said John Blackmore, when Kenton came round and told him the news. 'What do you call this? Another coincidence?' and the burly inspector was forced to admit that it was very strange.

'It simply amounts to this,' said the detective, 'when Boyle told me all that stuff on the morning he was executed he was speaking the truth.'

The Scotland Yard man looked at him incredulously.

'You surely don't mean that you believe it's his ghost?' he began, and Blackmore laughed.

'No, no,' he said. 'But he knew what he was talking about. Somehow or other he's left a legacy of death behind him. We're up against something, the origin of which we don't know anything about. What we do know is that it's potent.'

'I don't mind so long as it's something that's living,' growled Kenton. 'I thought for the moment you'd gone over to the ghost idea.'

John Blackmore shook his head.

'No,' he replied. 'There's nothing ghostly about bullets and knives. When people start using lethal weapons they are usually people of flesh and blood.'

'But why should anybody set themselves up as Boyle's avenger?' argued the inspector, rubbing his hand through his close cropped hair. 'What do they hope to get out of it?'

The detective lit a cigarette before replying.

'I don't know, Kenton,' he said at length. 'But there was some secret in Boyle's life that we know nothing about. If we did we should be in a better position to understand.'

It was the morning following the discovery of the dead body of James Lane, and they were seated in Blackmore's consulting room, the detective having barely finished his breakfast when Kenton had arrived.

'We couldn't be in a worse one,' grumbled the inspector. 'I don't know what you're talking about — secret in Boyle's life. He was all secret. There wasn't a scrap of paper, documents or anything at that house of his. Nothing, that is, that revealed who he was or where he came from.'

'That's the secret I'm referring to,' said John Blackmore. 'Who was he, Kenton? Boyle was merely a name, and it seemed to label him as well as any other, but who was he? What was his real name?'

The Scotland Yard man shrugged his shoulders.

'We tried hard enough to get him to tell us,' he grumbled, 'but he wouldn't say a word. An oyster was talkative compared with that fellow.'

'What happened to his house?' asked the detective thoughtfully.

'Shut up,' replied Kenton briefly. 'Trippers go down on Sundays and holidays and stare at it. Why?'

'I was wondering whether we'd overlooked anything there,' said Blackmore.

'I should think it was very doubtful.' The burly inspector shook his head. 'We combed the place thoroughly from cellar to garret.'

'I wasn't thinking of obvious places,'

answered the detective. 'It struck me that there might be some secret hiding place that we hadn't discovered.'

Kenton looked at his friend curiously.

'What makes you think that?' he asked.

John Blackmore blew out a ring of smoke and watched it slowly disperse ceiling-wards.

'Simon Boyle had occupied a great deal of my thoughts lately,' he said, 'and there's one very peculiar thing that I can't understand.'

'What's that?' enquired Kenton. 'Everything about the man was peculiar, but what are you referring to in particular?'

'What happened to his money,' said the detective. 'I've totalled up the various amounts that Boyle succeeded in swindling the banks out of, and during the ten years he was operating he got away with just over three quarters of a million. Where is it?'

The inspector sat bolt upright with a jerk.

'By Jove, Blackmore!' he cried. 'I never thought of that before.'

'So far as we have been able to trace,'

continued the detective, 'Boyle had no banking account. What then did he do with his money? Even allowing for the fact that he spent extravagantly there must be a considerable sum somewhere. What did he do with it?'

'He may have had an account for all we know,' said the inspector gloomily, 'or rented a safe deposit somewhere. He wouldn't have used the name of Boyle, naturally.'

'I very much doubt whether he would have used a bank or a safe deposit,' dissented Blackmore. 'You've got to look at it from Boyle's point of view. He was far seeing. The sort of man who would have made a good general, and although he was ultra clever there was always the chance of his getting caught as he was in the end. He would always have been prepared for a quick get-away, and with that in view, I think he would have kept his money somewhere where he could lay his hands on it at any moment of the night or day.'

'And you think it may be hidden at his house at Esher?' put in Kenton quickly.

Blackmore nodded.

'I think it's the most likely place,' he said. 'At any rate, I propose to go down there to-morrow and have another look round.'

There was a tap at the door, and the maid entered carrying a parcel.

'This has just come by registered messenger,' she announced.

Blackmore thanked her and took the parcel. It was a trifle smaller than a cigar box, and bore the name of a well-known Oxford Street Store on the brown paper wrapper. The detective turned it over in his fingers and frowned.

'What are you frowning at?' asked Kenton, surprised at the expression on his friend's face.

'I'm trying to think what this is,' said Blackmore. 'I can't remember ordering anything from this store. Besides, they wouldn't have sent it by district messenger, they would have their own delivery van.'

'I always find that if you want to know what's in a parcel it's a good idea to open it,' said the inspector sarcastically, and the detective smiled.

'Probably you're right,' he murmured, and taking a pair of small scissors from his pocket he cut the string and carefully removed the wrapper.

A white cardboard box was revealed. For a second Blackmore held it in his hand as though he was weighing it, and then with a quick movement he jerked off the lid.

Reposing in a nest of cotton wool was a round object covered with white tissue paper. He set the box down on the table and with the scissors gingerly snipped at the paper and pulled a large piece aside.

'Fond of apples, Kenton?' he asked in a changed voice, and the inspector attracted by his tone came over to his side.

In the centre of the white cotton wool reposed a small apple, but like no apple he had ever seen before for it bristled with steel needle points.

'Clever aren't they?' said John Blackmore, and there was genuine admiration in his voice. 'They must have used over a hundred needles and I'll bet there's death in every point!'

Kenton looked at the horrible thing, and his face was a shade paler. He, too, had been instrumental in bringing about the ruin of Simon Boyle and he was wondering when the unknown avengers were going to turn their attention to him!

5

The House of Shadows

'Very ingenious,' said Blackmore. 'I guessed it was something of that sort for it was heavy enough for a bomb. What would be more natural when one opened the package than to seize hold of this paper covered little ball.'

Kenton took out his handkerchief and mopped his forehead, which had suddenly become wet.

'My Lord!' he exclaimed. 'What a fiendish scheme. Do you mean that those needle points are poisoned?'

'I mean just that,' said the detective, calmly. He carefully put the lid on the box, tied the piece of string round it and locked it away in the drawer of his desk.

'It's useless trying to find out who gave it to the messenger boy,' he said. 'These people are too clever for that, it probably went through half a dozen hands.'

'But this is getting dreadful!' The Scotland Yard man's face was still pale. 'This is the third attempt they've made on your life.'

'Fourth,' corrected Blackmore, 'if you count the shots that were fired at me just after Boyle's execution. And I don't for a moment suppose this will be the last. The next few weeks are going to be dangerous, Kenton, for you as well as for me.'

The inspector had been thinking the same thing himself, but it didn't make it any the more pleasant to hear his own convictions put into words.

'Blackmore,' he said. 'We've got to get these devils before they get us!'

'I quite agree.' The detective went over to the mantelpiece and took a cigarette from the box that stood there. 'But it's not so easy as it sounds. They have the advantage of us, we don't know them but they do know us. It's like fighting in a strong light with your opponent in pitch darkness. They might be anybody, the man you sit next to in a bus. The man you pass in the street — either or all may be the power behind this conspiracy.'

Kenton rubbed his moustache irritably.

'But there must be some way of getting them!' he exclaimed, walking jerkily up and down in his excitement.

'There is, but it's rather a roundabout one,' replied Blackmore, 'and would take time. The way to get at these people is to trace back the history of Simon Boyle. Find out who he really is and all about him.'

'We tried to do that while he was waiting his trial,' said Kenton gloomily, 'and couldn't find out a darned thing. It's not very likely that we are going to be more successful now.'

'Unless I'm right, and there is a secret hiding place at the house at Esher,' remarked the detective quietly. 'If there is I think you'll find more than money there.'

'You mean papers relating to his past?'

Blackmore nodded.

'I should think it more than probable,' he said. 'Who's got the keys?'

'We have.' The Scotland Yard man stopped his aimless pacing. 'In fact, it's only two days ago that I withdrew the men that had been searching the place.'

'I wonder if you would let me have them,' said the detective. 'I've got an idea I'd like to have another look at that house.'

'I'll send them round as soon as I get back to the Yard,' promised Kenton, and shortly after took his leave.

John Blackmore had a lot of work to do. In spite of the menace of the unknown that stood at his elbow like the shadow of death, there were other cases that had to be attended to. None of them were very interesting, but they had to be looked into, and for the rest of the morning, and until late in the afternoon the detective was kept very busy indeed.

It was nearly six o'clock therefore when he brought his long bonneted Rolls to a halt outside the gates of what had been Simon Boyle's home. Getting out of the car he fastened the wide drive gate back, and then drove slowly up the gloomy avenue of chestnuts.

Presently he came in sight of the house, a low rambling building of red brick, with twisted chimneys, that nestled in a screen of trees. The windows were obscured by shutters, that gave the place a neglected, dead appearance, which even the trim lawns and flaming flower beds that flanked it on either side could not dispel.

For some unaccountable reason Blackmore felt a sudden chill as he switched off his engine and walked up the steps into the shadows of the porch.

Kenton had been true to his promise and had sent round the keys, and Blackmore selected the Yale front door key from the rest of the bunch and inserted it in the lock. How many times had Simon Boyle done just that very thing?

Almost as though somebody had spoken the words in his ear the thought flashed through the detective's mind, and it rather startled him for he was not a man given to mawkish sentiment, particularly over a callous murderer who had justly paid the penalty for his crimes.

The door swung open under his hand and he entered the gloom of the wide hall. There was an electric light switch near the door and he pressed it down.

The electric supply had not yet been cut off and a hanging pendant sprang into soft radiance. John Blackmore stood at the front door and looked about him. The place was very much as he had seen it last when he had assisted the police in their search, except that a thin film of grey dust lay over everything. The house was very still, uncannily still, like a human being that has held his breath in anticipation of something. It was unlike him to be fanciful, and yet the shadows on the great staircase and in the further corners of the hall seemed peopled with tangible shapes that moved and leered at him.

It was as though the spirit of the man who had made this place his home, who had gone about his dangerous and finally fatal work, brooded uneasily over the house.

'I'm getting childish,' muttered Blackmore to himself, and decided that he would start his investigating in the study. That was the most likely spot Simon Boyle would have chosen for a hiding place — if there were such a thing.

He knew the room, it was on the first

landing, and he began to ascend the softly carpeted stairs. It was very dark on the landing and he had to feel his way to the door of the room he wanted. It was half open, and pushing it wide he entered. The first thing that caught his eye was a ray of daylight streaming in through a crack in the closed shutters, and then, sliding his hand down the wall he found the light switch and flooded the room with light. A faint, musty smell came to his nostrils, and then he saw that somebody had been here before him!

The books had been removed from the shelves and left scattered on the floor in disordered heaps. The drawers gaped from the writing table, a portion of the carpet had been rolled back, the seats of the chairs ripped to shreds!

John Blackmore stroked his chin. Who had been responsible for the damage? Certainly not the police. Their search had been conducted thoroughly, true, but everything had been put back in its place, for one of the first rules that is instilled into the mind of an official detective is to avoid wilful damage. Who then?

There was only one answer to such a question. The unknown people who had taken it upon themselves to avenge the dead forger evidently knew there was something concealed in that empty house, and had been to look for it. Had they found what they had been seeking?

Blackmore closed the door. Advancing to the big writing table that stood in the middle of the room he looked down at the blotting pad. Here at this very table, in the still hours of the night Simon Boyle had sat and worked, his marvellous pen producing signatures so like the originals that the men whose names were forged could not tell them apart from their own.

For perhaps a minute the detective remained motionless, and then with a slight shrug of his shoulders he began a systematic search of the whole place. First he went to the walls, going over them inch by inch with a little jeweller's hammer that he took from his pocket, taking in each square yard on a definite plan, but not a hollow note sounded. Wherever the head of the hammer struck sounded good solid brick and mortar. He finished with the wall, having found nothing suspicious.

He turned his attention to the floor, the ceiling he ruled out. The slightest crack in its broad white surface would have shown with startling clearness.

The floor was of pointed wood parqueting, and the criss-cross blocks would have lent themselves admirably to the concealment of brick safes and secret hiding places. With meticulous care he went over the whole surface, looking for something that might afford a hidden spring. But again he drew a depressing blank, the wax polish in the cracks hadn't been disturbed for years.

Blackmore rose wearily to his feet and scratched his chin. Facing him on the wall hung a large picture, the painting of a man in ruffles, and the sardonic face leered from the canvas with a provocative and almost mocking smile.

'I wish you could speak, my friend,' muttered the detective. 'You've watched Simon Boyle, known all his secrets.'

There was only one place left for him to look as far as the study was concerned, and that was the fireplace. An ornate electric radiator had been fitted in place of the old open grate. He examined the tiles that surrounded this but there was nothing to reward his diligence. The mortar between them was firm and untouched. He tried the radiator itself to see if it would swing outward, and although it did the fraction of an inch it would not go any farther although he tried with all his might.

Panting, he gave it up at last, and getting to his feet wiped his streaming forehead.

And then he stood stock still, staring in utter astonishment. The picture of the leering cavalier was gone! The opposite wall was blank!

6

The Man Who Came In

John Blackmore stood rooted to the spot, too amazed to move. The thing was so obviously impossible that he could scarcely believe his eyes. Presently he recovered, and going over, stared up at the place where the picture had hung. Smooth and clear the panelling stared back at him. He got a chair and tapped the blank space. The hammer head rang solidly. With his eyes an inch from the beading he examined, pressed, pulled and pushed. Nothing!

To all appearances the wall was solid, and yet the picture had disappeared. It had been a full sized head and shoulders portrait and contained in a heavy gilt frame, protected by thick glass. It wouldn't have been an easy task for an ordinary man to have lifted it, and yet it had gone, spirited away without a sound!

A little chill sensation, like the trickling

of cold water ran down his spine. The room seemed suddenly to have become full of an icy wind, and he had a horrible feeling of being hedged in, surrounded by invisible eyes that followed his every action and yet remained unseen.

And then suddenly, in the midst of his imaginings came something tangible, the soft crunch of footsteps outside the house!

His muscles tensed, and he listened, straining his ears, but the sound was not repeated and he had begun to persuade himself that it was a hallucination when the lights in the room flickered and went out!

For some seconds he stood motionless in the pitch darkness, listening for a sound that did not come. Around him was a weird silence, a silence in which he could hear his own heart beats go thud — thud. Then he crept on tip-toe to the door and opened it. This time he did hear something — the soft pad, pad of rubber shoes from somewhere below. He was no longer alone in the house! Someone had come in!

He slipped his hand into his hip pocket and when he withdrew it he held an automatic.

The soft pad of the footsteps had ceased and he knew that they had become muffled in the thick pile of the carpet as their owner mounted the stairs. With every sense strung to its highest pitch he waited, alert and watchful.

The shuffling steps became audible again, drawing nearer and nearer.

Cautiously the detective drew back inside the room, and his left hand closed round the barrel of the electric torch. He had made up his mind to see what the unauthorised visitor to that disused house was like. Closer yet came that soft footfall, and then it stopped right outside the door!

The intruder was so near that Blackmore could hear the hiss of his breathing, but he came no further. They waited in the darkness, the unknown man outside and the detective inside, with only the thickness of the wall between them, and they each waited for the other to make the first move.

Blackmore was certain that the person who waited outside the door was aware that he had been heard — equally certain that he was aware that Blackmore was lying in wait for him. The detective smiled grimly in the darkness. If it was going to be a duel of patience he could play that game as well as anybody.

A minute passed — two — and still nothing happened. Except for that faint sibilant breathing — utter silence — an oppressive, menacing silence that was nerve wracking.

Blackmore felt an irresistible desire to spring out and challenge the man who waited there, but he repressed it, knowing that that was exactly what the other wanted. And then an idea occurred to him. When he had finished using it he had stuck the little jeweller's hammer in his breast pocket, and setting the torch down on the carpet without a sound he took the hammer from his pocket and pitched it through the half open door. It fell on the floor of the corridor outside with a thud, and instantly there came the sound of two muffled reports, and he heard the smack of the bullets as they struck the wall.

Blackmore's lips compressed into a thin line. There was no doubt about it, sudden death waited for him on the other side of that doorway. An acrid smell of burnt cordite drifted to his nostrils, but there were no more shots. The unknown had evidently guessed that he had been fooled, possibly had seen that the corridor was empty in the flash from the pistol.

The detective wondered what to do next. To attempt to cross the threshold was suicidal, but this vigil in the darkness was getting on his nerves. At the same time he fully realised that this was a state of mind on which the other was counting.

There was a faint creak of a loose board as the man outside shifted his position, and from the silence of the night without came the whirring of wheels on gravel. A car was coming up the drive!

'Can this be more of them,' thought Blackmore. 'And has the fellow been waiting for his friends to arrive, keeping me hedged up here until reinforcements come?'

It was an unpleasant thought. One had

been quite enough.

The approaching car drew nearer and stopped with a grinding of brakes. There was a pause during which Blackmore heard somebody walk towards the porch, and then a thunderous tattoo on the knocker echoed and re-echoed through the silent house!

From the unknown outside the door came a muttered oath, and the pad, pad of swiftly retreating footsteps. Blackmore's heart gave a bound of relief. Whoever it was who had come to the place it wasn't a friend of the mysterious intruder. There was nothing furtive about that banging on the front door, and from the exclamation he had given it had considerably alarmed the unknown.

Blackmore picked up the torch from the floor. If it was possible to prevent it he wasn't going to let the fellow get away without at least catching a glimpse of him. It had been impossible to move from the room while he had been stationed outside the door, but now was a different matter. The detective slipped out into the corridor and began noiselessly to creep in the wake of the retreating footsteps.

The summons on the front door was repeated impatiently, louder and longer, and it drowned the almost inaudible sound made by the other in his flight. He must have stopped, for without warning Blackmore suddenly bumped into him.

With a snarl the man swung round on him. There was a flash of flame and a pistol exploded almost in his face. So close was it that it singed his cheek and the bullet grazed his ear!

The next second Blackmore got a grip of the fellow's pistol wrist and with one sharp wrench sent the weapon thudding to the floor. The man fastened his other hand on the detective's throat, sinking his fingers deep into the flesh. Blackmore lashed out with his foot and caught his assailant on the instep. The man gave a cry of pain and fell, with the detective on top of him. He managed to keep his grip on Blackmore's throat, however, and the pressure tightened until the blood was throbbing in his head and he felt his senses reeling.

He tore at that steel-like wrist and tried

everything he knew to break that terrible hold. The floor seemed to give way beneath him, and together they went crashing and bumping down the stairs.

They landed at the bottom with a thud that almost knocked the breath out of the detective's body, but that strangling grip on his throat had relaxed. Before he could take advantage of it however, the other had wrenched himself free and scrambled to his feet. Blackmore heard him running towards the back of the hall and went after him, dragging his torch out of his pocket as he did so.

No longer in fear of the other's gun he pressed the button and sent a blinding ray of white light cutting through the darkness. The man had gone through a door that led to the kitchen, and Blackmore saw him, a gaunt figure in a long coat, fumbling at the chain of the back door.

He turned as the detective came up with him, and his eyes glaring hate through the holes in a black silk mask that covered his face.

'I'm going to see who you are, my

friend,' panted Blackmore, and clawed the scrap of silk from his face.

The movement gave the other his opportunity. Even as the detective's fingers ripped away the mask he picked up a heavy kitchen chair that stood by the door and brought it down with all his force on Blackmore's head.

The detective staggered and then collapsed, but in the instant that his senses left him he had seen the face of the unknown.

It was the face of Simon Boyle!

7

The Second Victim

John Blackmore came to himself and looked dazedly up into a large face that was bending over him — a large red face that gradually emerged from a sea of mist and revealed recognisable features.

'Hullo, Kenton,' he murmured faintly. 'How the deuce did you get here?'

'Don't talk yet,' grunted a familiar voice. 'Just lie still for a bit, you'll be all right in a minute or two.'

John Blackmore thought this was very sound advice and lay still. His head was throbbing unpleasantly and he felt rather sick, but his brain was clear.

He remembered that fleeting glimpse he had caught of the man who had struck him down. Simon Boyle! It couldn't be. It was impossible. Against all the laws of nature, for Simon Boyle was dead and buried — had been dead and buried for

57

nearly five weeks, and yet the features that had stared at him from under the mask were the features of Simon Boyle without a doubt!

He struggled up on to one elbow and tenderly felt the top of his head.

'All right now?' jerked Kenton, and the detective nodded. 'Then perhaps you'll tell me how you got like this,' went on the Scotland Yard man. 'I nearly knocked the door down trying to make you hear. Knew you hadn't gone because your car was still outside. I got fed up at last and smashed the dining-room window. What happened?'

John Blackmore told him, and he listened, his normally protruding eyes nearly starting from his head in amazement.

'Good Heavens!' he exclaimed at the end of the detective's story. 'It's incredible. Simon Boyle! You must have been seeing things!'

'I thought so myself when I pulled that mask off,' retorted Blackmore grimly. 'But there's no doubt about it, the man who came here to-night was the living image of the man who was hanged at Chelmsford Jail.'

'Do you think it could have been his brother?' suggested the inspector. 'If Boyle had a twin brother that would account for the resemblance.'

'I thought of that,' said Blackmore, 'although it seems a bit far fetched. The twin brother idea is all very well in books but it's very seldom you come across it in real life. Besides, there's nothing to show that Boyle possessed any living relatives. On the contrary, what little we have been able to learn about him tends to show that he lived alone and had no visitors.'

'Still, that doesn't prove that he hadn't got a brother somewhere,' objected Kenton. 'You're not going to try and make me believe that it was Boyle's ghost, are you?'

'Most certainly I'm not,' said the detective. 'I don't believe it myself. The man was much too substantial to be a ghost!' He touched the lump on his head. 'But you haven't told me yet what brought you down here.'

'I called round to Mecklinburg Square

and your secretary told me you'd gone down to Esher,' replied the inspector. 'So I ran along to see if you'd found anything.'

'I found something right enough,' said John Blackmore, 'but not the something I was looking for. Come upstairs into the study.'

He rose and Kenton was following with the torch when Blackmore remembered that there were no lights. He guessed that in order to put them out of order the unknown man had removed a fuse, and a little searching proved his surmise to be correct. The fuse box was behind the door giving access to the kitchen, and the fuse itself lay undamaged on the floor under it.

Blackmore put it back and the lights came on again at once in the hall. The light was also on when they re-entered the study, and the detective pointed to the portion of wall on which the picture had hung.

'Can you see anything wrong with that wall?' he asked.

Kenton looked at him suspiciously.

'No, I'm not pulling your leg,' he added

hastily. 'Have a close look at it and tell me if you can see anything that remotely resembles the entrance to a secret hiding place.'

The Scotland Yard man went over and made an examination that lasted for nearly five minutes. At the end of that time he shook his head.

'There's nothing here,' he said, 'except solid wall!'

'That's what I thought,' said Blackmore. 'But when I first entered this room this evening there was a heavy oil painting in a gilded frame hanging there!'

'By Jove! Of course I remember it,' cried the inspector. 'I wondered what was wrong. An ugly looking chap in ruffles.'

'Exactly,' said the detective. 'And while I was examining the fireplace with my back turned the ugly gentleman in ruffles disappeared.'

'Disappeared!' echoed the Scotland Yard man. 'What the devil do you mean?'

'Just what I say!' Blackmore pointed to the big electric radiator. 'I was pulling that about and I felt it move slightly — or thought I did — and when I looked round the picture had vanished!'

'Then the stove must work some hidden mechanism!' exclaimed Kenton excitedly.

'Yes, but what?' asked Blackmore. 'As you've seen for yourself the wall where the picture hung is as solid as the rest and there isn't the tiniest crack anywhere. I've tried pulling the beading but it's immovable.'

'Well, the stove must have done something,' argued the inspector. 'What did you do to it?'

Blackmore showed him.

'Let's see what I can do,' grunted Kenton, and stooped to tug at the radiator.

It was firm and refused to budge an inch. He tried pushing it but with the same result, and then he pulled it, first one side and then the other. But nothing happened. The opposite wall remained blank. There was no re-appearance of the picture of the leering cavalier.

Red in the face from his exertions the inspector straightened up.

'If that stove works the entrance to a

secret hiding place,' he growled, 'the man who designed it was a genius.'

'It undoubtedly does something,' said Blackmore. 'But as we don't know what or how, and we've tried everything, the only way will be to get a gang of men and strip the wall. Perhaps by that means we will find the missing picture.'

'I'll have it attended to first thing in the morning,' agreed Kenton.

'And talking of men,' said the detective, 'I think it would be a good idea if we stopped at Esher police station on the way back and got them to put a couple of men on to watch this place.'

'Do you expect that fellow to come back?' asked Kenton quickly.

Blackmore nodded.

'I think it more than likely,' he replied. 'Somebody's been here before to-night. Look at the state of the place. Your men didn't do that, did they?'

Kenton shook his head.

'I thought not,' went on the detective. 'These people are looking for something, probably the same thing as we are, and I don't want them to find it first.'

'I'll arrange to have the place watched,' said Kenton, and yawned. 'There's nothing more to stay for is there? I've had a heavy day and I shan't be sorry to see my bed.'

'No, we might as well be getting back.'

Blackmore took a last look round and switched off the lights. Making their way down the stairs they went out, shutting the front door behind them. The headlights of the police car that Kenton had driven down in were on, and flooded the darkness with light.

'Do you know where the police station is?' asked Blackmore as they walked down the steps.

'Yes,' said the inspector.

'Then you'd better go first and I'll follow your rear light,' said the detective, and went over to where his own car stood in the shadow.

He was just getting into it when he drew back with a startled exclamation. The driving seat was already occupied, but it was no living figure that slumped forward over the wheel, as Blackmore found when he raised the limp head!

'What is it? What's the matter?' Attracted by his cry, Kenton came running to his side.

'Look!' said Blackmore, and flashed his electric torch on the dead man's face.

'Great Heavens!' gasped the Scotland Yard man, and there was reason for the horror that filled his voice, for the man whose blood-stained face was revealed in the light was the foreman of the jury who had brought in the verdict against Simon Boyle!

8

Shots in the Night

'Blackmore,' said Kenton, and his voice shook. 'These devils make me almost afraid!'

John Blackmore said nothing, but his long lean face was set in hard lines and his mouth had become a mere slit, lipless and stern.

'How was he killed,' whispered the Scotland Yard man hoarsely.

'Stabbed — in the throat,' answered the detective. 'Rather a nasty business, Kenton. He hasn't been dead long either. There are no traces of rigor mortis yet. James Lane and now this fellow.'

'I wonder who will be the next?' muttered Kenton, wiping his damp forehead.

'There must be no next,' said Blackmore, and his tone was steely. 'Every precaution must be taken to prevent any further murders.'

'I wonder how they got him here and why?' murmured the inspector, and the detective shook his head.

'I don't know,' he answered, 'unless he lived somewhere in the neighbourhood. One thing, however, we can be fairly certain of. We are up against more than one person.' He frowned. 'You'd better go on to the police station while I wait here with the body. They can send along an ambulance and a doctor.'

Kenton nodded.

'All right,' he said. 'I'll go straight away.' He turned away and then hesitated. 'I suppose,' he remarked doubtfully, 'that you'll be all right. They're not likely to be lurking about.'

Blackmore shrugged his shoulders.

'I wouldn't like to say whether they were or not,' he said. 'But the local police have got to be informed, and somebody has got to stay here. We can't leave the body unattended. It shouldn't take you long — '

Ping!

The electric torch was snatched from

his hand and the echo of the report drifted towards them on the silence of the night.

Crack!

The second bullet took away Kenton's hat and a third hummed unpleasantly close to his head!

In two strides the detective reached the inspector's car and switched off the lights.

'Get down — behind here!' he rapped briefly, and pulled the Scotland Yard man under cover of the body.

A fusillade of shots followed, falling like hail against the metal coach work.

'They're firing from that belt of trees,' muttered Blackmore, 'and there's at least two of them. You can hear the difference in the sound of the pistols.'

Kenton grunted.

'I wish I could get my hands on the scoundrels,' he jerked venemously.

The detective slipped the pistol that he had knocked from the masked intruder's hand and which he had collected from the landing, out of his pocket.

'You stay here,' he whispered, 'and keep well under cover of the car.'

'What are you going to do?' asked the inspector.

'I'm going to see if I can't locate our friends,' answered Blackmore. 'They're somewhere in the middle of those trees on the other side of the lawn. With a little care I think I can worm my way through the shrubbery.'

'For Heaven's sake be careful!' said Kenton anxiously, but he was talking to empty space. John Blackmore had disappeared in the shadows.

He made his way cautiously into the thick bushes, and worked forward towards his objective without making a sound. Two more shots reached his ears as he crept on his way, and he smiled grimly for they sounded nearer and more distinct.

He had to move slowly now for the shrubbery was thick and tangled and he dared not risk making a noise. Presently the bushes began to thin out, giving place to scattered trees that formed the fringe of the copse from which the firing had come.

On the edge of the shrubbery he paused and peered into the darkness, hoping that he could locate his quarry by the flash of the pistols. But none came. He listened. There was nothing but silence; and then he heard something. The whirring hum of a starting car engine. It died to a dull murmur and then shrilled up into a whine that finally faded away as the car vanished in the distance.

Blackmore started forward again, keeping a sharp look out, though he was convinced that the departing car carried away the people he was seeking.

The other side of the belt of trees came out on a narrow lane divided by a wire fence. At one point he found that a portion of the wire had been cut away.

An examination of the rutted surface of the cart track — for it was little more — in the light of a match revealed a pool of black oil. A car had been standing there recently, had been standing there for some time. He dropped the match as it burnt down to his fingers. So this had been the way they had come. This accounted for the fact that he had heard no sound of a car. He wouldn't have heard it, for the study faced the other way. He went back to the place where he had left Kenton.

'Well,' said the inspector, and Blackmore informed him of what he had seen.

'They probably brought the body in the car too,' growled the inspector. 'Well, I suppose I'd better get off to the police station now that the excitement's over.' He crammed his hard bowler hat on his head savagely. 'That's ruined anyway,' he jerked. 'Bullet went clean through the crown.'

'Better your hat than your head,' said Blackmore. 'You can get a new hat.'

Kenton said nothing to this obvious truism, but climbing up behind the wheel of the police car, thrust at the self-starter. The engine broke to spluttering life, and with a word of farewell he disappeared down the gloomy drive.

John Blackmore lit a cigarette and seating himself on the running board of his own Rolls smoked thoughtfully, and waited for the Scotland Yard man's return. He kept a sharp look-out for any signs of the unseen enemy, but nothing happened. The quiet peace of the night remained unbroken, except for a distant train whistle and the soft rustle of the breeze that had sprung up.

Half an hour elapsed before he heard the throbbing of the engine and saw the lights of the returning car coming up the avenue of chestnuts.

Kenton was accompanied by the local inspector, two constables and a man in civilian clothes, whom Blackmore guessed was the doctor.

The inspector had evidently explained everything for after a word of greeting the doctor made his examination, the police car being turned so that its headlights provided sufficient light. He wasn't long over the job. In less than two minutes he looked up.

'He was stabbed in the neck with a narrow bladed knife,' he announced. 'It severed the jugular and he practically bled to death!'

'About how long has he been dead?' asked Blackmore, and the doctor pursed his lips.

'Couldn't say exactly,' he answered. 'Somewhere about three hours I should think, but that's as near as I can tell.'

'That's good enough,' said Kenton, and turning to the waiting policemen: 'Get this poor fellow out of Mr. Blackmore's car and we'll run through his pockets.'

They obeyed, lifting the sagging form and laying it gently on the gravel of the drive. The Scotland Yard man went rapidly through the clothing, putting what he found on his handkerchief which he had spread out beside the body.

It was not a formidable heap. There was a wallet of well worn leather, a gold watch, a cigarette case, some loose change and a bunch of keys. That was all. Kenton picked up the wallet and peered into the pockets. There were a few visiting cards in one, and he pulled these out.

'James Fletcher,' he said, and nodded. 'I remember his name now, I couldn't recall it at first.' And then. 'Good Heavens. He lived in Balham!' He glanced at Blackmore, amazement on his face.

'Well, what about it?' remarked the detective. 'Why shouldn't he have lived at Balham?'

'Why the devil did they bring him here? Why didn't they kill him nearer his home?'

'They probably waylaid him somewhere, killed him, and then conceived the idea of leaving the body in Boyle's old home as a dramatic gesture,' said Blackmore. 'These people are nothing if not dramatic in their actions. It would appeal to them. When they discovered that I was in the place they improved on their original idea, and while you were attending to me in the kitchen they put the body in my car.'

'Who are these people you're talking about?' enquired the local official.

'I wish I could tell you that, Inspector,' said Blackmore, 'but I can't. All I can say is that for some reason of their own they're taking it into their heads to wreak vengeance on everybody who was connected in bringing Simon Boyle to justice.'

'It's a wonder that they 'aven't 'ad a go at Mr. Mallin,' remarked the inspector.

'He was the judge what tried Boyle,' unnecessarily. 'And I said to me missus at the time what a curious coincidence it was.'

'What was?' asked Blackmore.

'Why, that 'e should 'ave been livin' within a stone's throw of the man who sentenced 'im to death,' was the reply. 'Mr. Mallin lives over there,' he pointed to the right. ''Illbrow 'is house is called. You could see the chimney back of them trees if it wasn't dark.'

John Blackmore made no comment on this piece of information but it was news to him and he made a mental note of the judge's address for use in the very near future.

Kenton had finished looking over the contents of the dead man's pockets, and now, under his orders the body was placed in the back of the police car.

'I don't think there's any more to be done to-night,' he said to Blackmore. 'I'm leaving the two constables in charge, and after the inspector and I have seen the body put into the mortuary I shall go home.'

'I think I shall go home now,' said John Blackmore, 'unless you want me for anything, I'm feeling pretty tired.'

'Yes, you go along,' said the Scotland

Yard man. 'There's no need for you to come with us.'

The detective said good night to the others and got into his car. He repressed a shudder as he took his place behind the wheel, remembering the last occupant of that seat, and then letting in the clutch sent the big Rolls gliding down the drive.

Three o'clock was striking as he reached London, and it was nearly half-past by the time he had put away the car and walked the short distance from the garage to the flat. He was both tired and hungry, and helping himself to a stiff whisky and soda, he munched biscuits while he undressed. Two minutes after his head had touched the pillow he was asleep.

The whirring of the telephone woke him, and sitting up sleepily he reached for the instrument. As he lifted the receiver he glanced at the clock and saw that it was a little after eight.

'Hullo,' said Kenton's voice. 'That you, Blackmore? I'm speaking from Esher. Can you come down right away?'

'What's happened?' demanded the detective, now fully awake.

'I can't tell you over the phone,' said the Scotland Yard man. 'I'm at the police station now, but I'll meet you at Boyle's house. All I can say is that our friends have been busy again.'

There was a click as he rang off, and Blackmore leaped out of bed. By eight-thirty he was bathed, shaved and dressed, and by ten o'clock was once more standing in the study of the dead forger's home.

'They came again during the night,' said Kenton. 'Look!'

John Blackmore looked. The picture of the leering cavalier had once more appeared on the wall, but there was a difference. It now hung at an angle, half projecting into the room and half in the dark cavity that was behind it.

'It moves on a central pivot and the back is panelled like the rest of the room.'

'How did they get in?' asked John Blackmore. 'Where were the two policemen, asleep?'

'They were when we found 'em,' said Kenton gruffly. 'Drugged and unconscious. They're recovering now in the local infirmary!'

9

A Visitor to Mr. Justice Mallin

'Of course,' said John Blackmore, 'they got away with what they came for?'

Kenton nodded.

'Yes,' he replied gloomily. 'You can see for yourself the place is empty.'

The detective walked over to the yawning cavity. It was slightly larger than the frame of the picture, and the carved beading of the panel hid the join when the painting revolved into its place. Behind was a shallow cupboard lined with steel and containing a row of steel shelves. Blackmore wondered how it was he had failed to hear the hollow when he had been tapping but soon discovered the reason when he saw that there were two panels at the back of the picture and that the place between them was filled by a sheet of steel over an inch thick. That undoubtedly would have deadened any sound of hollowness and given the illusion of solid wall.

He peered into the wall safe, for that was what it was on an elaborate scale, but there was nothing except ridges of dust on the shelves. They lay in regular lines, and showed plainly where packages had been stacked, but there was nothing left, the shelves had been cleared completely.

Blackmore came back to Kenton.

'How does the thing work?' he asked, and the inspector pointed to the electric stove.

'You nearly found out yourself last night,' he said.

The detective stopped in front of the big fireplace.

'You press that screw head,' explained Kenton, and put his finger on one of the screws that held the silvered frame together, 'and then pull the stove towards you. It moves about an inch, and that swings the panel round so that the picture is on the other side. You must have touched the screw accidentally when you were examining the stove and that's why the picture disappeared. It locks, however, in that position unless you also switch on the current that normally lights the heater. When the stove's pulled out, however, it doesn't heat the coiled wires, but works the mechanism operating the safe door instead.'

'Most ingenious,' murmured the detective. He twisted the switch to 'Off' and pressing the screw, pushed the radiator back.

It moved easily and then locked, and looking round he saw that the picture of the cavalier hung in its normal place against the wall, and there was no sign of a hidden hiding place.

Pressing the screw again he pulled the stove towards him. It slipped an inch and stopped, and looking up Blackmore saw that the picture frame had swung completely round and that now there was only blank panelling! Without turning he felt for the switch and twisted it to the 'On' position. Instantly the section of panel moved and opened until it was at right angles, revealing the opening behind.

'Most ingenious,' said Blackmore again, and rose to his feet. 'Well, they've forestalled us. Whatever there was concealed in there, and it was possibly money and documents, might as well be at the bottom of the sea for all the help it's going to give.'

Kenton pursed his thick lips and frowned.

'They must have come back just before dawn,' he said. 'It was the relief men who discovered that there was something wrong when they came on at five o'clock, and the local inspector phoned me. There's going to be trouble over the Fletcher business.'

'There'll be more trouble if there are any more deaths,' said Blackmore. 'I think a list ought to be made of the people closely or even remotely connected with the trial and execution of Boyle, and they should be warned and if possible placed under observation. It's my opinion that they'll turn their attention to Judge Mallin next, and I think it would be just as well to call and see him and prepare him for what to expect.'

'I agree with you,' replied the Scotland Yard man. 'What makes you think, though, that he'll be the next?'

'Up to the present,' said Blackmore, 'they seem to be following some sort of order. I was the first they went after, and I was instrumental in bringing about Simon Boyle's arrest. The next victim was the prosecuting counsel. Then last night, the foreman of the jury. It's not stretching the imagination too much to suppose that the judge has been marked down to follow. That would be the order of precedence. Prosecuting counsel, foreman of the jury, the judge!'

'And after that comes Mellish the hangman,' remarked Kenton, 'if they're following the method you suggest.'

'Exactly,' replied Blackmore. 'So I think that Mallin ought to be warned.' He glanced at his watch. 'I shall go up to Hillbrow now,' he went on. 'Are you coming with me?'

Kenton shook his head.

'I've got to wait here for the local man,' he said. 'See you later.'

Blackmore walked up to Hillbrow. It was a lovely morning, with just enough breeze to make the heat of the sun comfortable without being excessive, and the road that led up to the judge's house was shady and enticing.

Hillbrow was an older house than the dead forger's. Half timbered and almost hidden by a thick screen of trees, and Blackmore found Mr. Justice Mallin taking his ease beneath a spreading yew tree on his trim lawn. The long vacation had just begun and Mr. Mallin had not yet left for his usual holiday abroad.

He laid down the newspaper he had been reading and looked up in surprise when the black clad butler announced Blackmore.

'Hullo, Blackmore!' he exclaimed. 'What's brought you here? Sit down my dear fellow, sit down. Cramp — another chair.' With the air of a High Priest the butler produced a chair and Blackmore sat down.

'Now,' said the judge, producing a cigar case and holding it out invitingly, 'tell me the reason for this visit. I'm delighted to see you, of course, but I cannot flatter myself that this is anything but a business call?'

The detective helped himself to a cigar and lit it. Puffing out a cloud of odiferous smoke he proceeded to tell Mr. Mallin why he was there.

The judge's lean, heavily lined face assumed an expression of amazement as he proceeded, and when he had reached the end of his story Mr. Justice Mallin looked at him for some seconds in complete silence.

'It's incredible — unbelievable!' he exclaimed at length. 'Of course, I read something about the death of Mr. Lane in the papers, but I never for a moment associated it with that fellow Boyle — incredible.'

'All the details, except the bare finding of the body, were suppressed at the express wish of the police,' said Blackmore. 'It was considered best in the interests of the police not to let it become known that there was any suggestion of a conspiracy behind it.'

Mr. Mallin nodded his grey head gravely.

'It's absolutely without precedence,' he said. 'Monstrous! And but for the fact that it is you who have told me I should pooh-pooh the whole thing and put the deaths of Lane and Fletcher down to some other reason. Even now I can scarcely credit it. A feud of vengeance carried out by some persons unknown seems more reasonable to fiction than real life.'

'There is a very small line dividing what man imagines and what actually takes place,' said John Blackmore. 'Few stories have yet been written that have not found their counterpart in life.'

'I suppose in a way that is true,' admitted the judge. 'But to revert to this unpleasant business. What do you suggest that I should do? What do you advise?'

John Blackmore blew a cloud of smoke slowly from between his lips, and watched it drift from the shadows into the sunlight.

'Without wanting to alarm you in any way,' he said. 'I believe that you are in very great danger from these people. They are not likely to end their atrocities with the killing of Fletcher, and I therefore suggest that from now onwards you take the most stringent precautions. Do not go out alone and allow me to arrange that this place is placed under police protection.'

Mr. Justice Mallin frowned, and his strong face expressed his disapproval.

'Is that necessary?' he asked. 'I must say that I dislike the idea of a police guard.'

'I think that it is very necessary,' said the detective decisively. 'At all costs, any further murders must be prevented and I'm afraid, Mallin, that even without your consent I must insist that you are properly looked after.'

The frown deepened between the judge's brows, and for a long time he made no reply. Then his forehead cleared.

'I have found a solution to the difficulty,' he said. 'That's if you are agreeable.'

Blackmore looked at him enquiringly.

'What is your suggestion?' he asked quietly.

'That you come and stay with me here as my guest!' was the reply. 'I shall be delighted to have your company and you will be able to see that I am immune from attack. Therefore we shall kill two birds with one stone. What do you say?'

John Blackmore considered the idea rapidly, and came to the conclusion that it was a good one. It established him near to Simon Boyle's home, and also placed him in the position of getting to grips with his unknown adversaries, for he was certain that sooner or later they would concentrate their attention on the judge, and in that event he would have a greater chance of outwitting them if he was on the spot. Quickly he made up his mind.

'I shall be very pleased to accept your invitation,' he said, and Mr. Justice Mallin beamed.

'Excellent!' he exclaimed. 'Come as soon as you like. I — '

He broke off as the sombre garbed figure of the butler appeared carrying a silver salver. The judge took the envelope that lay on it and with a word of apology to Blackmore, ripped open the flap. The detective saw his face change as he read the contents, but he said nothing until the butler had passed out of earshot. Then he handed the letter to Blackmore.

'Read that,' he said shortly, and the detective glanced at the single sheet of paper. It contained five lines of typescript and ran:

'You sentenced Simon Boyle to death and in doing so sentenced yourself. On the tenth day of this month that sentence will be carried out. You have ten days to live, make the most of them!'

* * *

There was nothing else, no signature, date or address.

'What do you make of that?' asked the judge, and though he spoke lightly his face was a trifle paler.

'I make this of it,' said Blackmore. 'The murders of the others were heralded by no warning letters. Why should they have changed their tactics with regard to you?'

'Well?' Mr. Mallin regarded him interrogatingly. 'Why should they?'

'I'll tell you,' replied the detective, and his voice was stern. 'This letter was sent with one purpose, to fix your mind upon a date — to give you a false sense of security until the tenth dawns. It is between the tenth day of the month and this moment that the period of danger lies!' He folded the letter and handed it back to the judge. 'I'm rather glad I accepted your invitation,' he said!

10

An Evening at Hillbrow

John Blackmore arrived at Hillbrow an hour before dinner. He had refused Mr. Mallin's pleadings to stay to lunch on the excuse of urgent business and in view of this, that worthy man would have been considerably surprised at the detective's subsequent movements, for after stopping for a brief word with Kenton, Blackmore had driven back to Mecklinburg Square and promptly gone to bed where he had slept solidly until just after four. That night and every night during his stay at Hillbrow were going to be very wakeful for John Blackmore, for he had decided that it was at night that the danger would come.

On his return to Hillbrow he was shown to his rooms by the dignified butler, and he had finished dressing and was brushing his hair when there was a tap at the door and his host entered.

'I've got one or two people coming to dinner,' he said. 'Neighbours of mine and my bank manager. It is a good plan to keep in with one's bank manager.' He laughed. 'What I came to ask you is whether you wished to be introduced as yourself or whether you are going to take some other name — '

'There's no necessity for that,' broke in John. 'You can rest assured that the people we are up against know all about my presence here.'

He picked up his dinner jacket and slipped it on.

'You know,' said the judge, 'I once met Simon Boyle when he was living here — as you are aware he called himself Colonel Andrew Wilton — it was in the post office and we exchanged some remarks about the weather. I don't know why I tell you this but I've been thinking a lot about Boyle since this morning and happened to recall the incident.'

A suspicion that had flashed through Blackmore's mind now became a certainty. In spite of his seeming unconcern

Mr. Justice Mallin was afraid! He was talking for the sake of talking, and his feeble excuse for coming to see Blackmore was inspired by the uneasiness of being alone.

He remained talking about nothing in particular until he was called to welcome the first of his guests.

A few minutes later when the detective entered the drawing room he found a group of people and was introduced to a Mr. and Mrs. Evans and their daughter Sonia, a tall pale girl, with large dark brooding eyes with a hint of concealed sorrow in their depths. Mr. Evans was not unlike the judge in face and figure, indeed they might easily have been mistaken for brothers, a fact which Mr. Mallin commented on with amusement. But it was Mrs. Evans who interested Blackmore more than any of the others. A tall slim woman with a lined yellow face and almost black eyes.

She had in her youth obviously been of great beauty, and although that had faded with age her personality was still striking and vivid. She dominated the room — would have made her presence felt in a far greater crowd, and when she spoke, her voice was low and peculiarly sweet, like the babbling of spring water.

'Are you the Mr. Blackmore?' she asked, moving over to the detective's side, and the detective replied that he was. 'Your profession must be very interesting,' she went on, looking at him steadily with her magnetic eyes. 'I have always been interested in crime, and I'm afraid I am an insatiable reader of the newspaper reports of trials. Let me see. Weren't you connected with the local sensation — the Boyle man?'

Blackmore admitted that he was. In spite of her efforts to be charming he had taken an almost instantaneous dislike to her, and it was with something approaching relief that he turned away with a muttered apology as the judge called him to introduce him to a fresh arrival.

'I think you have met Mr. Stacey before,' remarked his host, and Blackmore looked with surprise into the smiling face of the immaculate young man who had been in the United Bank at Colchester, on the morning of the arrest of Simon Boyle!

Mr. Stacey extended a limp hand.

'Met under deuced unpleasant circumstances,' he murmured. 'Deuced unpleasant. See that wretched policeman even now in my sleep — horrible.'

He drifted away to pay his respects to the Evans', and Blackmore was left with the judge.

'I'd no idea you knew Stacey,' he said in a low voice. 'Does he live around here?'

Mr. Justice Mallin nodded.

'Yes,' he replied. 'He's got a bungalow about a mile away. Curious coincidence, isn't it?'

John Blackmore thought it was a very curious coincidence, and decided to keep an unusually sharp eye on Mr. Stacey.

When Simon Boyle had shot the unfortunate plain clothes man, Blackmore had wondered how the pistol had got into his possession, for a search of his clothes had revealed no bulging of the pockets such as there would have been if he had carried the heavy weapon about on him. Could the explanation be that he had had the automatic passed to him by Stacey when that young man had taken a hand in the fight? If so, then Stacey was undoubtedly one of the mysterious people who had taken upon themselves the task of avenging Boyle's death!

John Blackmore's thoughts were interrupted by the arrival of the last guest. It was Mr. Hollins the bank manager, a stout and jovial man with a large face and a large smile and a large expanse of waistcoat.

Cramp, the dignified butler, with the air of one who was conferring a tremendous favour on everyone, announced that dinner was served, and Blackmore found, when they took their seats at the polished table in the dining-room, that he had been placed between Mrs. Evans and the rather vacuous looking Mr. Basil Stacey. Immediately opposite him was the judge's confidential secretary, who came in a few minutes late with an apology that he had been completing some important work.

The dinner was excellent, perfectly chosen and perfectly cooked, and yet by no stretch of imagination could it be called a success. Mr. Justice Mallin did his best to keep the conversation flowing, but although Blackmore and Hollins seconded his effort, the Evans' and the immaculate Stacey failed to respond.

The girl, whose Christian name Blackmore learned was Sonia, scarcely opened her lips, except for the purpose of eating, throughout the meal, and she did very little of that, merely picking at her food and keeping her eyes on her plate. Mr. Evans attempted to join light heartily in the small talk but it was a feeble attempt. His remark faded away incoherently as though he was thinking of something else and his thoughts had got the better of him.

These people seemed to be constant visitors at Hillbrow and to be great friends of the Judge's, for he addressed Mrs. Evans and her daughter by their Christian names, and Blackmore wondered whether he had told them of the reason for his presence and the receipt of the threatening letter, and whether this was the possible explanation of his distraction. It seemed likely for the stout banker was in the highest spirits and kept up a running fire of really amusing stories and anecdotes, that fell rather flat.

The Judge's young secretary, Harry Morris, was also rather subdued. He could scarcely take his eyes off the pale girl and Blackmore sensed that he was rather keen in that quarter.

The meal came to an end at last and coffee was served in the drawing-room. After that they played bridge — a game that the detective detested — until it was time for them to depart to their various homes.

Although Mr. Mallin had referred to the Evans' as neighbours, Blackmore discovered that they were anything but, in the strict sense of the word, for they did not live in Esher, but a good ten miles away and had driven in by car.

'I hope we shall meet again,' said Mrs. Evans as she said good-bye to the detective, and there was a look in her dark eyes that Blackmore could not quite fathom.

He puzzled over it as he made his preparations for the night, and he was unpacking some rather peculiar things that are not usually found in the suit-cases of people visiting friends, when it suddenly came to him what that expression had indicated.

Malignancy! That was it. For a second while she had been speaking sheer naked hate had blazed in the velvet blackness of her eyes!

Blackmore paused with a long cardboard cylinder that he had just taken from his bag, in his hand. Yes, there could be no mistake. In spite of her honeyed words Mrs. Evans' tell-tale eyes had given her away. But why in the name of goodness should she hate him? They had, so far as Blackmore knew, never met before, and although he could have understood dislike — he himself had taken a dislike to the woman at sight — there had been more than dislike in that momentary flash.

And then one of those extraordinary 'hunches' came to him, those sudden intuitions that he never ignored, and which had done much to place him in the front rank of his profession. Mrs. Evans hated him because he had been the means of bringing Simon Boyle to the death house!

11

The Noose!

John Blackmore had much to occupy his mind as he sat at the open window of his bedroom and gazed out across the dark grounds. The night was hot and airless, and faintly in the distance he could hear the rumble of thunder. Away to the south a jagged ribbon of blue flame split the sky. A storm was coming up following the almost tropical heat of the last few days.

Sitting there alert and watchful, the detective heard the household gradually settling down for the night. There came the dull sound of a clanking chain and rasping bolt as Cramp, the butler, locked up, and then the soft pad of his feet fading away, and after that silence.

Blackmore could see very little outside for the night was very dark, and lighting a cigarette he gave himself up to his thoughts.

He could give no reason why Mrs. Evans hated him because he had brought Simon Boyle to justice, but he was as certain of the fact as if that extraordinary woman had said it in so many words. And if that was the case, then she must be connected with the people who were avenging themselves on those who had brought about the dead forger's downfall. It seemed absurd, but the detective was too sure of his instinct to allow reason to swamp it, and there had been no imagination about the look he had surprised in her eyes when she had said good-bye.

Again came the question that had hammered at Blackmore's brain ever since the beginning of this extraordinary case. Who was Simon Boyle? In the answer to that lay the whole solution of the mystery. What was his real name? The files at Somerset House had been searched without result. Boyle had been a myth, a nobody. He worked on his own, had run no gang, and yet somewhere in the background of his life there lurked people who were willing to commit murder in order to avenge his death.

What had poor 'Harry the Dip' known that had sealed his doom, and what was the job he had been asked to do and who had asked him to do it?

Blackmore's thoughts whirled round in a chaotic circle, coming back every time to the unanswerable question — Who was Simon Boyle?

One thing at least seemed concrete, that the focal point from which everything emanated was near at hand. It was more than a coincidence that Basil Stacey, the immaculate fop who had flung himself into the struggle at the Colchester Bank, should live within a stone's throw of the house that had been the property of the man to whom Blackmore firmly believed he had handed the pistol in the moment of his extremity.

Stacey, therefore, was one of the unknown group against whom he was pitted. Were the Evans' also part of that murderous gang?

Without definitely being able to say yes or no, Blackmore felt that his first evening at Hillbrow had not been wasted. Apart from his belief that Mrs. Evans had something to do with the business, which was based on nothing more tangible than a fleeting expression, there was at least a possible line in Stacey. He would find out from the Judge in the morning how long he had been acquainted with these people and what he knew about them.

The storm was getting nearer. The mutter of thunder had increased, and the lightning was incessant. Not a breath of wind stirred and the atmosphere was oppressive. Blackmore wondered if the night would yield any results.

That Mallin was in danger he knew. When would the blow be struck? If his idea was correct concerning Stacey and Mrs. Evans, and that would naturally include Evans as well, and possibly the girl Sonia, they had ample opportunity for getting at the Judge. But Blackmore was pretty certain that whatever attempt was made would be made at night. They wouldn't risk anything during the day, and the fact that they were aware of his presence at Hillbrow would make them ultra cautious.

The time passed slowly sitting there in the darkness and twice in the flicker of the lightning he thought he saw something move over in the shadow of the belt of trees that flanked the lawn, and although he strained his ears no sound came except the rumble of the thunder, and he concluded that his imagination was playing tricks on him.

And then he did hear something!

It was just after a distant clock had chimed the hour of two that he heard it and it came from inside the house, the faint, almost inaudible noise of a closing door!

Blackmore was across the room and at his own door in three swift strides. Opening it gently he passed out into the dark gloom of the corridor and listened. Silence! Nothing but the measured tick of the grandfather clock in the hall.

For five minutes he stood motionless, but he heard nothing. And yet a door had closed somewhere, stealthily.

He was debating whether he would go down and see if he could find out the source of that first sibilant sound when a silenced whispering reached him!

It was drowned almost at once in a peal of thunder, but he had heard the direction. It came from outside. He tip-toed back to the window and keeping within the room, tried to catch the vague sound again. Presently he heard it, the low tones of two voices, speaking softly and hurriedly, a man's and a woman's! They were quite close somewhere in the path that ran underneath his window, and they seemed to be arguing fiercely. The woman seemed to be doing most of the talking and the detective only heard the deep tones of the man occasionally.

He tried to make out what was being said but could only make out an inaudible mutter.

Who were the speakers and what were they doing in the grounds of Hillbrow at that time?

Cautiously he extended his head over the broad sill but he could see nothing. The murmur, however, still floated up to him and it came from the left. Craning his neck Blackmore waited for the next flash of lightning that would enable him to see who these unknown whisperers were. It seemed an eternity before it came and then the whole lawn and path was lit up in a blue glare. Blackmore caught the black silhouette of two figures standing beneath his window. For one brief instant he glimpsed them, but he failed to recognise either, and then something soft touched the top of his head. He looked up sharply, felt something slip round his neck and tighten on his throat.

Throwing up his hands he clutched wildly at the strangling cord. He couldn't breathe and he was being dragged slowly but inexorably upward.

He tore frantically at the rope, the blood throbbing in his temples, his lungs bursting, but steadily, remorselessly he was being pulled off his feet!

In a last effort, with his senses reeling, he gripped at the taut line above his head, taking his weight on his arms, and then with a jerk he was hurled completely out of the window. He swung there helplessly, his hands slipping on the smooth rope. A few seconds more and his full weight would rest on the noose round his neck.

A tremendous thudding boomed in his head and flashes of fire danced before his eyes. He heard somebody laugh, and then everything went blacker than the night!

12

Cartwright Takes a Hand

Harry Cartwright arrived at Esher just before dusk. He had received explicit instructions from Blackmore that afternoon, and with his usual thoroughness proceeded to carry them out. A short way from the drive gates of Hillbrow he dismounted from the motor cycle that had brought him from London, and wheeling the machine along until he came to the narrow lane that Blackmore had described he hid the cycle under a tall hedge and continued on foot. The lane ended in a barbed wire fence, close to which was a five barred gate that led into a ploughed field.

He ignored the gate and carefully climbing the fence found himself in a small plantation so thickly planted with trees that the trunks almost touched one another.

He was now inside Mr. Mallin's property, and moving forward he eventually reached a dense belt of shrubbery beyond which was a gaily coloured flower bed, and beyond that again the lawn. He was now facing the house and could see the lights in the windows gleaming through the gathering dark.

Blackmore had particularly stipulated that he should take every precaution against being seen by any of the household. His job was to keep a sharp look-out for anybody who might enter or be lurking about the estate after nightfall, and the detective had also arranged that in the event of his requiring assistance within he would light a red flare in his window. He had, during his visit of the morning, discovered that all the bedroom windows overlooked the lawn.

Harry was not particularly enthusiastic with the part that had been allotted to him. He foresaw a long and rather dreary vigil that would probably end in nothing, and he preferred something more exciting, but Blackmore's orders had been explicit, and had to be obeyed.

He explored the shrubbery until he found a place from which he could obtain a clear view of the house while he himself remained completely screened from observation, and here he took up his position.

The dusk deepened to darkness, and, presently, after what seemed an eternity, he heard the noise of a car engine and the whining purr of a high powered motor as it sped down the drive and faded into the distance.

This, although Cartwright didn't know it, was the departure of the Evans'. Shortly after this the lights in the windows began to go out one after the other, and the house became almost invisible against the blackness of the night.

It was very still, utter silence, except for the crackling of twigs as some furry or feathered creature moved stealthily through the wood behind him, and then, far away in the distance, came the rumble of thunder.

'That's going to be very pleasant,' thought the secretary, as he heard it. 'A good old storm and I shall be soaked to the skin.'

A flicker of lightning lit up the face of the house like a picture flashed for an instant on a screen, and Cartwright shifted his position and stretched his cramped limbs.

One o'clock struck — half-past — two. The silence and the oppressive heat was making him feel drowsy, and he had very nearly dropped into a doze when suddenly he was alert and wakeful. From somewhere out of the darkness had come the sound of a footstep, he heard it crunch softly on the gravel and peered in the direction from which he thought the sound had come. He could see nothing, but the soft crunch of the footsteps were still audible, and then heard voices, low toned and whispering. Who was abroad at this hour?

The footsteps stopped but the voices went on, drawing nearer and Cartwright concluded that the speakers had left the gravel path and were walking across the lawn. They were within a few feet of where he lay concealed, and as they passed he was able to catch a word or two here and there of what they said. It was a woman who was speaking.

'There's no risk . . . attract his attention, that's all . . . Look out the window . . . He will do the rest.'

Her companion grumbled something that the secretary couldn't catch, and then they went beyond his hearing.

Whose attention are they going to attract, thought Cartwright, and prayed for another flash of lightning that would enable him to catch a glimpse of the speakers. It came, but they were too far away for the lad to distinguish anything but two dim figures walking towards the sleeping house.

He noted the direction they had come, however, and leaving the shrubbery, began to creep cautiously in their wake. It was essential that he should see who they were. Blackmore would never forgive him if he allowed such an opportunity to pass.

Another flash of lightning shed a blue white glare over everything and Harry flattened himself out on the lawn and hoped that he had not been seen. Evidently he had not, for the voices continued slightly louder than before. He crawled forward and then suddenly he heard another sound that made his flesh creep. A horrible, gasping, choking sound!

The whispering voices ceased abruptly, and retreating footsteps rapidly faded in the distance.

The gasping, groaning sound went on, and added to it was a scraping rasp.

Cartwright almost ran forward. Something devilish was going on. The dreadful sounds were coming from above and then in the fitful gleam of another flash of lightning he saw the swinging figure that hung at the end of a rope against the white stone work of the house — saw and recognised the discoloured face of John Blackmore!

The secretary's brain worked rapidly. There was not time to rouse the house. There was only one chance and he took it. Dragging the torch and his automatic pistol from his pocket, he focused the bright white beam on the slender rope, and then, with set teeth, took careful aim!

Keeping his finger pressed on the trigger he emptied the magazine. He saw the splinters of stone fly from the wall as the bullets struck, and the rope frayed and parted as two of his shots cut through the strands.

Blackmore fell with a crash into the soft mould of the flower bed beneath, and the next second Cartwright had torn the strangling noose from his neck. But he had only been just in time. The detective's face was purple and the rope had cut a deep red circle in the flesh of his throat. His tortured lungs drew in great whistling draughts of air, and presently he opened his eyes. He tried to speak but no words came, only a hoarse croak.

'All right, sir. Lie still for a bit,' said the secretary. 'You'll feel better in a minute or two.'

The sounds of the shots had aroused the house. Lights flashed up in the windows, and there was a rattling of bolts and the butler appeared, a grotesque figure in a flamboyant dressing gown.

'What's the matter? What's happened?' he called. 'Who fired those shots?'

'I did,' snapped Cartwright. 'Mr. Blackmore has been attacked. Go and get some water!'

'But who are you?' began the butler. 'How did you — '

'Don't waste time asking questions,' said the secretary impatiently. 'Go and do as I tell you!'

Cramp was hesitating when a second figure came out of the door.

'What is it, Cramp?' asked a voice. 'What was all that firing?'

'Something has happened to Mr. Blackmore,' said the butler, but got no further for with an exclamation of alarm Mr. Justice Mallin hurried to Cartwright's side.

'Blackmore hurt?' he asked anxiously. 'Good Heavens! Don't tell me that — that — ' His voice trailed away. He was obviously afraid to put the question that trembled on his lips.

'It's not serious as it happens, but it easily might have been,' said Cartwright, and briefly explained.

The Judge listened aghast.

'But this is dreadful!' he exclaimed, when the secretary had finished. 'Dreadful! An awful thing! Are you quite sure Mr. Blackmore is unhurt?'

Cartwright nodded.

'He'll be as right as rain in a few minutes,' he answered. 'I've asked your butler to get some water twice, but he evidently prefers to admire the landscape.'

Mr. Mallin swung round.

'Cramp! — do as you're told!' he ordered angrily, and the butler slunk away.

He returned after a slight delay carrying a glass of water, and Cartwright held it to Blackmore's swollen lips. The detective drank greedily.

'That's better!' he gasped, huskily. 'By Jove! My throat hurts!' He put up a shaking hand and tenderly felt his neck.

Mr. Justice Mallin started to say something but his words were drowned by a tremendous peal of thunder, and then the rain started.

Cartwright helped Blackmore to his feet and leaning on the secretary's arm the detective made his way shakily indoors. A little later, seated in the dining-room, they sipped the hot coffee that Cramp had hurriedly made.

'It's a monstrous thing,' remarked Mr.

Mallin pacing agitatedly up and down, in his somewhat scanty attire. 'How did they manage it?'

'The rope came from above,' said Blackmore. 'They must have had somebody planted on the roof.'

The secretary related the scraps of conversation he had heard as the man and the woman had passed him, and the detective nodded.

'A very effectual scheme,' he said, 'and but for your timely intervention, Harry, would have been quite successful. They guessed that the sound of voices under my window would make me look out and they had everything prepared. Clever!'

'But who are these people?' cried the Judge. 'How did they know which room you were occupying? How did they know you were here at all?'

John Blackmore looked at him queerly. Should he express in words his vague suspicions concerning the Evans' and Basil Stacey? He decided not to, at least, not for the present. He would gather a little more information first — try and find some concrete evidence to support his theory before committing himself.

'Their information seems to be pretty complete,' he replied evasively. 'They appear to know most things.'

When the storm had passed over and in the cold grey light of dawn, he accompanied his secretary on a voyage of exploration. Against the side of the house they found a light ladder reared, and there were marks on the grass to show where it had been dragged from a gardening shed.

'That's the way the man with the rope went,' commented the detective, and climbed the flimsy structure.

The roof of Hillbrow was covered with red tiles, but in the centre, immediately over the room that Blackmore had occupied was a seven foot space of flat leads. There was a trap door in the centre but he found that it was fastened from within. There was no doubt that this was the place from which the murderous plan had been carried out, for in his flight the would-be hangman had left the frayed ends of the rope hanging over the gutter. It was a very ordinary clothes line, and valueless as a clue, nor was there anything else that suggested the identity of the unknown. Blackmore went back to Cartwright who was waiting below.

'I suppose you didn't see enough of the two people to be able to recognise them again?' he said, and the secretary shook his head.

'What was the woman's voice like?' Blackmore persisted. 'Low and soft, rather sugary?'

'I couldn't say,' replied Cartwright. 'They were both speaking in whispers, and you can't distinguish between one person whispering, and another.'

The detective nodded. He hadn't recognised the voices, either, but he had a shrewd suspicion that the woman had been Mrs. Evans, and there and then he decided on a bold stroke. Immediately after breakfast he would pay a visit to the Evans' and see if he could surprise them into giving something away. And having made that decision he had only one thing that troubled him. What had been the meaning of that softly closing door he had heard?

Was there somebody within Hillbrow who was in league with the people who had taken upon themselves the avenging of Simon Boyle? And if so, who could it be?

13

Crooks in Conference

Mr. Charles Evans stood looking out of the window of his large and airy breakfast room, his lips pursed in a soundless whistle, watching a dancing shaft of sunlight on the velvety lawn, and only a faint tiredness in his eyes proclaimed the fact that he had not been to bed that night. Presently he turned to the woman who was seated at the table sipping a cup of coffee.

'That fellow has got as many lives as a cat,' he said cheerlessly.

The woman raised her eyebrows but went on sipping the steaming fluid without replying.

'Who would have thought he would have wriggled out of that trap last night.'

He came over and pulling a chair out impatiently, sat down.

'Well, he did! And that's the end of it,'

she snapped. 'It's our fault, we ought to have guessed that he would have had somebody watching the house from outside. It's lucky that neither Basil nor I were caught.' She set down her empty cup. 'The next time, though, we'll take no chances. We'll make certain!' She spat the words out viciously.

'Have you heard from Mark this morning?' he asked, and she nodded.

'He couldn't say much. It was risky speaking at all,' she replied, 'but he wants to see you at Basil's bungalow this afternoon.'

'Why?'

She shrugged her shoulders.

'Money,' she said briefly. 'There was not nearly so much as there ought to have been in Simon's safe. He must have been spending money pretty freely before — ' she left the sentence unfinished.

'Does Mark propose that we go on with that scheme then?' asked her husband a little dubiously.

'Yes! Why not?' she demanded.

'Well, don't you think we're attempting too much?' he put the question hesitantly as though not quite sure how it would be received.

'Getting cold feet?' she sneered, and his face flushed.

'No, only — ' He shook his head. 'We ought to attend to one thing at a time. If we are going to finish the job of getting back on all the people who — who were the cause of Simon's death let's get that over before we tackle anything else.'

'If we are?' she took him up quickly. 'What do you mean by that? There's no question of our backing out of that, is there? Or perhaps you'd like to.'

'Well, if you must know,' he flared up suddenly, 'I think it's stupid — staining our hand with blood for no useful purpose!'

'You're getting squeamish!' she retorted contemptuously. 'You always were a weakling, Charles. You'd better tell that to him. He'll know better how to answer you than I can.'

Charles Evans paled and he pulled at his lip.

'I was only giving you my opinion,' he said, 'and there's no need to make a song about it. I know he wouldn't agree with me.' He changed the subject abruptly. 'If we are going on with that scheme we shall have to find somebody to take the place of 'Harry the Dip'.'

'That shouldn't be difficult,' said the woman. 'Only for this time, for Heaven's sake don't be such a fool as you were over that business. If Basil hadn't acted quickly we should have found ourselves behind steel bars. As it was your carelessness resulted in poor Simon being caught.'

'And I haven't been allowed to forget it,' snarled Evans. 'How was I to know the darned little crook was going to follow me to Simon's place? I haven't second sight!'

'You haven't even got first,' she said. 'You and Sonia would make a fine pair.'

'What's that about me?'

The pale girl with the dark eyes had come into the room silently. She looked even paler than she had done on the previous night. There were purple shadows under her eyes and the lids were swollen as though she had slept little.

Mrs. Evans shrugged her shapely shoulders.

'I was saying that you and your father

would make a good pair,' she answered. 'You're both getting chicken-hearted.'

'Getting!' the girl laughed mirthlessly. 'I've got! I'm sick to death of all of it! Sick of dead men and blood! Ugh!' She shuddered.

'Well, you'll have to put up with it a little longer,' retorted the woman, rising to her feet. 'And what have you got to grumble about anyway? You have all you want, don't you? Money to spend, clothes to wear — '

'Yes!' Sonia Evans swung round and faced her, her eyes blazing. 'And where does the money come from? Everything I touch, spend, or wear has the smell of the tomb! My education was paid for with stolen money. Oh yes, I've got everything I want except a clear conscience.'

'You're hysterical!' snapped her mother. 'You were never like this until you got friendly with that Morris fellow. He hasn't had a good influence on you.'

'You leave him alone,' said the girl. 'At least he's honest. He hasn't got much money but what he has got he got honestly.'

'You sound like a tract,' sneered Mrs. Evans. 'Why don't you join the Salvation Army!'

Sonia said nothing, but with a little sob she almost ran out of the room, slamming the door after her.

'Why don't you leave the girl alone,' muttered Evans. 'She's not any too well — '

'She's all right,' asserted his wife, 'there's nothing the matter with her except that she's got the Sunday School bug biting her. That, and love's young dream are all that's the matter with her. We shall have to watch her, though — people in her mood are dangerous.'

'We shall have to ease off Hillbrow a bit,' began Charles Evans, but she interrupted him.

'Ease off nothing!' she said. 'We're going through with the original plan. Mark is determined.'

'He must be mad!' The man felt for a cigarette and lighted it. 'It's nothing short of insanity to attempt anything with Blackmore there.'

'Blackmore's not going to be there

long,' she said meaningly. 'And anyway, there's nothing to be afraid of so far as he's concerned. As personal friends of the Judge's we're the last people he's likely to suspect.'

She broke off with a quick look of caution as a step sounded in the corridor and then a tap on the door.

'Come in,' said Mrs. Evans.

A trim maid entered.

'Will you see Mr. John Blackmore?' she asked, and Charles Evans' face went grey. For a moment even the stronger-minded woman was taken aback, but she quickly recovered herself.

'Show him into the drawing-room,' she directed. 'I'll join him almost immediately.'

The maid departed and as soon as she had gone Evans stepped hurriedly across and shut the door.

'What has Blackmore come for?' he demanded hoarsely. 'What's the reason for this visit?'

'How on earth should I know,' she replied, but her sallow face was lighter in colour. 'He can't suspect anything.'

'Then why do you think he's here? To enquire after our health?' snarled Evans, his lips twitching.

The woman eyed him and her mouth curled disdainfully.

'For Heaven's sake pull yourself together!' she rasped in a low voice. 'And keep out of the way. If he sees your face it would be as good as giving him a signed confession!'

By a supreme effort Evans controlled his quivering nerves.

'Well, you must admit it's rather a shock,' he said. 'It's funny that he should come all the way from Hillbrow.'

'Remarkably amusing,' she said sarcastically. 'I find the greatest difficulty in stopping myself from laughing.' She moved towards the door. 'Anyhow, the best way to find out why he is here is to see him.'

She left the breakfast room and walking with a firm step crossed the hall. Outside the door of the drawing-room she paused and braced herself for the interview, for in spite of her manner in front of her husband there was an unpleasant feeling of fear in her heart.

She was all smiles as she sailed into Blackmore's presence.

'Mr. Blackmore! This is an unexpected pleasure.'

The detective had been standing by the window and at her entrance he turned and bowed over the hand she held out to him.

'The pleasure is on my side, Madam,' he said courteously.

'Won't you sit down?' She waved towards a deep easy chair, and when Blackmore was seated: 'I hope that this visit doesn't mean there has been any trouble at — Hillbrow?'

She looked at him steadily as she put the question.

'Why should you think there has been any trouble?' he asked.

'Well, the Judge told me about the letter he had received, and then you being there — ' She laughed. 'Well, naturally, we put two and two together.'

'And discovered that they added up to the conventional four,' said the detective easily. 'How nice it is when they do that, isn't it? Now I have got two and a fraction of a shadowy third, and I'm hoping to be able to make those add up to four.'

'You speak in riddles.' She sat on the arm of the settee. 'I don't know what you mean.'

Without offering an explanation Blackmore went off at a tangent.

'Did you sleep well last night?' he asked.

'Very well, thank you,' answered Mrs. Evans, with a slight elevation of the eyebrows. 'Why?'

'I was merely wondering whether the storm disturbed you,' murmured the detective.

'Did it disturb you?' she enquired quickly.

He shook his head.

'It didn't disturb me for the very simple reason I wasn't asleep,' he replied.

'Do you suffer from insomnia?' she smiled enquiringly.

'I always suffer from insomnia when I stay in strange houses,' said John Blackmore gravely, 'and I therefore usually spend the night at my bedroom window.'

'How very dull for you.' She stifled a yawn. 'The time must pass very slowly. What do you do to amuse yourself?'

'I just watch and listen,' said the detective.

'And what do you hear?' Her tone was indifferent — rather bored, but he noticed the quick rise and fall of her breast as she breathed faster.

'Sometimes I hear quite a lot.' He looked straight into her peculiar magnetic eyes. 'For example, I heard you last night, Mrs. Evans. What were you doing in the grounds of Hillbrow at two o'clock?'

14

Blackmore Throws Down the Gauntlet

Watching, Blackmore saw her catch her breath, and felt a little thrill of satisfaction that his bluff had come off. He was certain now that Mrs. Evans had been the woman whose voice he had heard in the small hours of the morning.

She had not expected that sudden question, and her reaction to it had given her away. But still, to know it himself and to be able to prove it in a court of law were two totally different things. She recovered herself quickly.

'Really, Mr. Blackmore,' she said, in well acted amazement. 'You must suffer from hallucinations as well as insomnia. I was not at Hillbrow at two o'clock. I was in bed and asleep.'

'Then perhaps you can account for the fact that my secretary who was watching in the grounds, saw and heard both you

131

and Mr. Evans. You passed within a yard of him?'

Blackmore had made a mistake, he realised it as soon as the words left his lips, and he saw the sudden little gleam of triumph that lit up her sombre eyes. Charles Evans had not been her companion, and she knew that he was bluffing.

'Have you taken the trouble to come all the way here in order to make these ridiculous charges?' she sneered. 'Of course, there is not a word of truth in them. Neither my husband nor myself left this house after we returned at eleven o'clock last night.'

'Can you prove that?' asked Blackmore sharply.

'Can you prove that we did?' she retorted.

Blackmore was silent. He couldn't prove it and she knew he couldn't. He had hoped by springing a surprise to trap her into an admission, and he had failed.

'I'm afraid — to use a slang expression — that you are barking up the wrong tree, Mr. Blackmore,' she went on smoothly. 'You are wasting your time. You are fighting people whose brains are just a trifle cleverer than yours, and you are trying to save your reputation by accusing innocent people because you have failed to find the guilty ones.'

'Do you think so?' The detective raised his level brows a fraction of an inch. 'Even the cleverest people make mistakes, Mrs. Evans. Simon Boyle was clever but he finished on the trap with a rope round his neck!'

He made the reference to the dead forger deliberately, watching her to see the effect of his words, and he was satisfied. Her yellow face remained expressionless, but she could not control her eyes. They blazed with sudden malignancy although when she spoke her voice was low and silky.

'Really, Mr. Blackmore,' she said. 'I'm not interested in the criminals you have brought to justice. If you have nothing further to say I'm afraid I must ask you to excuse me, I have some business to attend to this morning.'

She rose to her feet and John Blackmore followed suit.

'At present I have nothing more to say to you, Mrs. Evans,' he said quietly, 'except this. The inside of Chelmsford Jail is uncomfortable, but it is Paradise compared to Holloway Prison. And even women are hanged in this country!'

He got home!

The woman's yellow face flushed darkly, and he heard her laboured breathing.

'Be careful how you threaten me,' she hissed. 'It's only by luck that you are still alive. Last night — '

She stopped abruptly, biting her lips.

'What do you know about last night?' snapped Blackmore quickly.

'I know nothing!' She forced herself to regain her composure. 'I'm sorry I lost my temper, Mr. Blackmore, but you annoyed me.'

John Blackmore walked towards her until he was less than a foot from that sallow lined face.

'Last night — or to be more correct — this morning, an attempt was made on my life,' he said, speaking slowly and distinctly. 'It failed, owing to the quickness of my secretary, who is at present waiting for me outside this house. In spite of the fact that you assert that you were asleep at the time you know as much about that attempt as I do!'

'I'm not going to listen to your insults any longer!' She swept past him to the door. 'You must be mad! That's the only excuse I can make for your monstrous conduct. I've already told you I know nothing of what you are talking about.'

'I dislike having to tell a woman I don't believe her,' retorted the detective, 'but in your case that is nothing more than the truth!'

'Leave my house at once!'

Mrs. Evans flung open the door and Blackmore bowed. Reaching the threshold he paused and looked her straight in the face.

'I'm leaving now, but one of these days I shall come back, and I shall not come alone.'

She licked her dry lips.

'What do you mean?' she whispered.

'You know very well what I mean,' said the detective. 'But if you like I will put it more plainly. I was no very great friend of

'Harry the Dip's' but I have sworn to get the people who killed him!'

'I'm not interested,' she muttered huskily.

'You will be intensely interested,' he said, 'in the trial and the verdict and the eight o'clock walk that ends in the death house and eternity. I'm sure Simon Boyle found them all extremely interesting.'

'You — you devil!' Mrs. Evans almost choked over the words, and she swayed against the doorpost.

'It sounds rather crude the way I put it, doesn't it?' said John Blackmore harshly. 'But death *is* crude, so is murder. The police officer whom Boyle shot at Colchester found it crude, so did 'Harry the Dip,' and James Lane and poor Fletcher, and so will you and the people with you when your time comes!'

He left her leaning against the door, one hand at her throat, and the naked hate that shone from her eyes sent a shiver down his spine. But he was satisfied with his morning's work. He had carried the war into the enemy's camp and thrown down the gauntlet.

What he had suspected before was now a certainty. The Evans' were the people behind the mist, the unknown hand that was raised against those who had brought Simon Boyle to justice. Blackmore knew now but he couldn't prove it. There was nothing that could be taken before a jury. Nothing even that would provide sufficient evidence for arrest. But he had shaken Mrs. Evans' nerve, and that had been precisely his object in calling that morning.

He had proved over and over again in the course of his career, that if you can get a crook in a panic, get him on the run, he will usually do something stupid, make a slip that eventually puts him in the dock, and he hoped that the same thing would happen in this case.

From now on the Evans' would be carefully watched, and if they made one false move it would lead to their undoing.

John Blackmore was whistling softly to himself as he got into the Judge's car that was waiting for him with Cartwright at the wheel, and he was still whistling as they glided up the drive at Hillbrow.

It is a debatable point, however, whether he would have felt so cheerful could he have seen what was going on in the house he had just left, for Mrs. Evans was seated at the telephone in her private room pouring the account of the recent interview into the ears of the man who was listening at the other end of the wire.

'There is no doubt that he suspects,' she concluded. 'What shall we do?'

For ten minutes she listened while the person she had been talking to replied, and when she finally hung up the receiver and went downstairs to find the scared and frightened Evans she was feeling almost cheerful, for the voice that had come over the wire had suggested a plan that sealed the doom of John Blackmore and gave the detective less than a week to live!

15

The Judge Disappears

The rest of the morning passed uneventfully, and it was not until lunch time that anything happened to disturb the serenity of the summer day.

The storm of the night before had been succeeded by scorching heat and a cloudless sky. It was ideal weather, but John Blackmore was in no mood to enjoy it. There was a menace overhanging Hillbrow in spite of its bright flowers, trim hedges and shaven lawns, a menace that was the more potent because of its intangibleness.

The detective, it is true, was fairly certain that the Evans' were at the bottom of the attempt on his life, but it was only his own suspicion. He had no proof, nothing that was likely to convince a court of law, or even an ordinary policeman, and they knew he had no proof.

In his interview with Mrs. Evans he

had succeeded for a second in probing beneath her guard, but the mask had been resumed with lightning speed, and that momentary glimpse of fear that he had surprised had been quickly concealed. But it had been there, and no woman who was entirely innocent would have acted in the way that Mrs. Evans had. He had played a bold stroke in tackling the enemy in their own stronghold, and if he had gained nothing more he had at least had the satisfaction of proving for his own private benefit that his suspicions were not without foundation.

The next step was to discover concrete facts that would warrant the police taking action against these people, and that was not easy. They were not burglars. They planned carefully and in the crimes that had already been carried out they had not left the vestige of a solid clue.

Blackmore wondered who was the brains of the outfit. It was certainly not Basil Stacey. He might be very good at obeying instructions but he was not the organiser. His personality was all wrong for that, and Blackmore knew something about personality. And it was not Charles Evans, he had not sufficient strength of character. Mrs. Evans was capable, she possessed everything that the others lacked, an iron will and the necessary imagination to work out her plans. And yet if it was Mrs. Evans who was at the head of the conspiracy what was the object? Why should she set herself up as Simon Boyle's avenger? What possible motive could she have? Whatever it was it was a strong one.

John Blackmore had planned a trip to London after lunch, and he made a mental note to add to the list of things he already had in his mind; namely, to find out all he could regarding the Evans' past in the hope that it would supply him with the link he was searching for.

He occupied part of the morning in a close examination of the flat roof from which the killer had dropped the noose. There were plenty of signs of the man's presence, blurred footprints in the grime and two long scratches where his feet had slipped, but nothing else, and none of the prints was sufficiently clear to be helpful in discovering his identity.

After his inspection of the roof Blackmore turned his attention to the grounds. But here he met with no better reward. The rain had destroyed all marks — if marks there had ever been, and although he thought there might have been a possibility that he had missed something when he and Cartwright had looked in the uncertain light of dawn, in the powerful midday glare that possibility was remote.

Remembering the noise he had heard from within the house, that stealthy sound suggestive of a closing door, he questioned the servants closely and separately, but none of them had left their rooms during the night, and again he was forced to admit that he had drawn a blank.

He rejoined his secretary in the garden.

'I'm going up to Town after lunch,' he said. 'Keep an eye on things while I'm away.'

'When do you expect to be back?' asked Cartwright.

'I hope to be back in time for dinner,' replied Blackmore. 'Anyway, I shall be back before nightfall.'

'Do you expect anything to happen to-night?' asked Harry, after a short silence, and the detective shrugged his shoulders.

'It's impossible to tell with some people,' he said. 'They're capable of anything, and we mustn't forget that Mallin is in just as much danger as we are. Probably more so at the moment, for having made their attempt against me and failed they may turn their attention to the judge.'

He didn't know it at the time, but his words were prophetic.

'It's the most extraordinary case we've ever tackled,' said Cartwright. 'There's something weird about it when you come to think about it. Simon Boyle is dead — dead and buried, and yet he is still able to wreak his vengeance on the people who were connected with his idea — just as he said he would. It's uncanny!'

'If you are beginning to get the ghost idea into your head, you can get it out again, quickly. There's nothing ghostly about the people we are up against. They are good solid flesh and blood — solid enough to hold that rope last night, anyway!' He fingered his throat reminiscently.

Cartwright flushed.

'I wasn't suggesting that there was a ghost at the bottom of it,' he protested. 'I was remarking that it was peculiar.'

'I'm quite aware that it's peculiar without being told,' snapped Blackmore.

He was not in the best of tempers which to a certain extent was excusable. He was more or less edgy, being faced by a problem that no matter how he looked at it presented a blank wall, and Cartwright understood this and so took no notice. He knew that Blackmore was not so much impatient with him as at the forced inaction and endless waiting. He felt rather the same way himself.

The detective wandered down to the rose garden, and paced up and down thoughtfully until it was time for lunch, and Cartwright accompanied him in silence, realising that under the circumstances silence was more than golden.

When they got back to the house for lunch they found Cramp in the hall looking uncertainly about him with a troubled expression. His face cleared as Blackmore and his secretary came in, and he hurried forward.

'Have you seen the judge, sir?' he asked.

Blackmore shook his head.

'Not since early this morning,' he replied.

The butler's frown returned.

'I thought he was with you in the garden,' he said. 'That's where he told me he was going.'

'I haven't seen him at all,' replied the detective, and there was a sharp note of anxiety in his voice. 'When did he go out?'

'An hour ago, sir,' replied Cramp. 'He asked where you were and when I told him I'd seen you in the garden he went out.'

'Perhaps he changed his mind and came back again,' suggested Cartwright. 'We were down in the rose garden and he wouldn't have seen us from the front door.'

'If he was in the house, sir, he would have come in answer to the luncheon gong, I've rung it three times. Besides, I've looked in the study and in his bedroom, and he isn't in either.'

'This is serious,' snapped Blackmore, and his face was set and grim. 'We must make definitely certain that he's not anywhere in the house and then we must search the garden. Something may have happened to him.'

He and Cartwright and the scared butler began a methodical search of Hillbrow. Taking it in sections they searched it from attic to cellar without leaving a square inch unexplored, but there was no sign of Mr. Justice Mallin. He had completely disappeared.

With a feeling that was almost akin to despair in his heart Blackmore turned his attention to the grounds. If anything had happened to Mr. Mallin he felt that he could never forgive himself. He had been there to protect the judge, and the man had been spirited away under his very eyes. He had failed in his duty. It had been a gross piece of carelessness on his part to have left the judge for so long alone, but he had felt confident that nothing would happen in the daylight.

They searched the grounds as carefully as they had searched the house, and with the same result, there was no trace of the judge anywhere.

'What on earth can have happened to him?' cried Cartwright as they stood hot and dusty in the centre of the lawn. 'Can he have gone out anywhere?'

'He would have gone after lunch or else he would have come back in time for it,' said Cramp. 'The master's most particular about meals, will have them on the second.'

'I don't think he's staying away of his own free will,' said Blackmore, with compressed lips. 'I'm afraid the enemy has struck while we were least expecting the blow to fall!'

'But — Good Heavens, sir! What could they do in broad daylight?' exclaimed Cartwright incredulously. 'I could understand it if he'd been shot from the woods, but completely spirited away — how could it have been done? We should have heard if he'd cried out.'

'Perhaps he didn't cry out,' said Blackmore. 'Perhaps they didn't give him the chance to cry out!' He swung round on the butler. 'Are you sure you didn't see which way he went when he came out to look for me?' he asked.

Cramp shook his head.

'No, sir, I'll swear to you I didn't,' he answered. 'I'd tell you if I had and gladly. I was busy decanting the wine for lunch and didn't wait, sir.'

In spite of the fact that Blackmore was suspicious of everybody there was a ring of truth in the butler's voice that forced him to believe the man. Whoever may have been concerned with the disappearance of Mr. Mallin he felt certain that Cramp was innocent.

They stood on the lawn in the hot glare of the sun completely puzzled, and then Blackmore, who had been frowning down at the grass looked up.

'You stay here with Cramp,' he said to Cartwright. 'I'm going down to the drive gate to see if I can find any traces there. We've exhausted all the grounds and if there's not a sign of a clue on the roadway we shall have to get in touch with the police and form a search party to cover the woods.'

He set off quickly with long, swinging strides down the winding drive, his face grim and set. This was a development he had not been prepared for and he made a silent vow that he would not rest until he had found the judge, alive or dead!

If Mr. Justice Mallin had been inveigled into the power of these people he had very little hope of finding him alive. There was no hesitation about their methods, they acted swiftly. And after all, Mallin was the person who was chiefly responsible for the death of Simon Boyle.

Reaching the end of the drive John Blackmore looked up and down the road. It was deserted, a baked stretch of white dust in the sunlight. He stooped and examined the surface by the drive gate but he could find nothing. There was no mark sufficiently distinct for him to deduce anything from it. It was true there were several tracks in the gritty dust. He could make out at least two tyre prints and the wheels of a wagon, but the road was a public thoroughfare though little used, and there was nothing suggestive in these. None of them had stopped at all close to the drive, that was certain, and he extended his examination to further along.

It was about fifty yards away that he found traces of one of the cars having stopped. The back wheels had left furrows in the loose surface where they had skidded on the application of the brakes, but the car had evidently gone on again and there was nothing else to be seen.

Blackmore tried the opposite direction but here he drew a complete blank altogether, and he was in the act of retracing his steps and turning into the drive once more when a figure appeared round the bend in the road, a figure that was swaying drunkenly from side to side.

As it came nearer it waved its hand feebly and called in a hoarse croak that barely reached the detective's ears, but Blackmore had seen the face and hurried forward to meet the staggering man.

It was Mr. Justice Mallin!

16

The Man in the Car

The judge almost collapsed as John Blackmore reached his side and the detective had to grip him by the arm to prevent him from falling.

He was covered from head to foot with dust and looked as if he had been rolling in the roadway.

'Blackmore!' he gasped. 'I've had a dreadful experience! A dreadful experience! They nearly had me! It's a wonder I'm alive!'

He stopped breathlessly and hung on to Blackmore's arm. He was obviously nearly at the end of his strength, and as he opened his mouth to speak again the detective stopped him.

'You can tell me all that's happened presently,' he said. 'At present you'd better come back to the house and have a stiff drink and some food. That'll soon put you right again.'

Mr. Mallin was too worn out to argue, and allowed himself to be led in silence up the drive.

Cartwright and Cramp were still waiting on the lawn, and they greeted the arrival of Blackmore and his companion with dumb surprise.

'Where did you find him?' asked the secretary when he had recovered from his astonishment.

'I didn't find him, he found me,' replied the detective. 'Here, Cramp, take your master upstairs and let him get all this dirt off himself. We'll join you at lunch, Mallin,' he added.

The judge nodded weakly and disappeared into the house with the butler.

'What happened to him? How did he get into that state?' asked Cartwright.

'I haven't the least idea,' answered Blackmore. 'He was staggering along the road on his way back to the house when I saw him, and all he said was that he'd had a dreadful time. I wouldn't let him say any more. When he's had a wash and a change I've no doubt we shall hear the story from him.'

They did!

Between mouthfuls of food Mr. Justice Mallin related his experience.

'I had written one or two letters,' he said, 'and as they were rather important I thought I'd post them at once. There's a box at the end of the drive as you have probably noticed. Putting the letters into my pocket I came down to the hall and seeing Cramp there I asked him where you were. He said that you were somewhere in the garden, so I decided that I would post the letters and then come and hunt you up. Last night had given me a nasty time and I don't mind admitting that I wasn't feeling too well.'

He paused and took a sip of wine.

'I walked down the drive and slipped the letters in the box, and then as I was turning away a car came along the road, passed me and stopped. The driver leaned out and called something. I didn't hear what he was saying, but, thinking that he had lost his way and wanted some directions, I went up to the car. He asked me the quickest way to the railway station and I was pointing it out to him when somebody seized me from behind and slipped a chloroformed pad soaked over my mouth and nose.

'I struggled as much as I could, but the person who held me was as strong as a lion and although I tried to hold my breath and not breathe in the fumes of the drug I had to give in in the end, and I don't remember any more.'

He stopped dramatically and looked from one to the other.

'You'd never seen the driver before, of course?' said Blackmore.

The judge shook his head.

'No,' he answered. 'He was a complete stranger to me. A short, ugly, wizened faced man. At least, as near as I could tell he was short, I never saw him out of the seat. However, to continue,

'I recovered from the effects of the drug and found myself in the car. It was not moving but had been turned off the main road and driven down a side lane. It was barely half a mile away from the point where I had been attacked and in front of the grounds of the house that used to belong to Simon Boyle!'

He waited, evidently waiting for Blackmore to make some comment, but the detective remained silent, and after a pause the judge continued.

'The driver of the car was still sitting in his seat, and the man, I presume it was the same who had administered the drug to me, was standing by the side of the car talking in a low voice.'

'Did you see his face,' interrupted Blackmore.

'Yes, I saw his face,' replied Mr. Mallin, and his voice dropped and shook slightly. 'I will come to that later. The man finished what he was saying to the driver — I couldn't hear a word but I believe he was issuing instructions for the other kept nodding — and then came round to the window and looked into the car. I thought it was best to pretend that I was still unconscious and closed my eyes quickly.

'It was the car moving that made me open them again and I discovered that we were backing out of the lane. The driver was still behind the wheel but the other had gone. We backed out into the main road and turned in the direction of Esher.

They had evidently taken it for granted that I was still unconscious for no attempt had been made to secure me in any way, and as the car gathered speed I began to rack my brains for a way of escape. Keeping my eyes fixed on the back of the driver's head I cautiously tried the doors. They were locked and I could see that the windows had been screwed up. The screws had been put into the panes clumsily and were plainly visible.

'I couldn't see any possible chance of getting out of that car without attracting the driver's attention, and that would have been fatal. He was a wiry looking fellow and more than a match for me, and he was also probably armed.

'I had nearly given up hope when I saw that the hood of the car was a leather one, fastening in the middle of the roof with metal clips, like the hood of a taxi, and my heart jumped. If I could push back those clips without the knowledge of the man in front, and this was possible because a glass partition divided us, I could let down the back of the hood and take a chance of jumping out. There was a good chance of breaking my neck but I am sure that death awaited me at the other end of the journey anyway, so the risk was worth it.

'To cut a long story short, Blackmore, I managed it. I got those clips undone without arousing the suspicions of the driver, pushed the leather hood down and climbed over the back.

'We were travelling at about thirty miles an hour I should think when I dropped into the road, and although I turned a complete somersault I wasn't hurt beyond being bruised all over. I got to my feet and ran as I haven't run since I was a boy at school. I heard the squeak of the car brakes behind me and was in an agony of fear lest it should turn and overtake me, but the driver must have been scared that there might be somebody else come along the road for he didn't try to catch me.

'I ran until I was all in and then just as I felt like dropping I saw that I was back at my own house and caught sight of you.'

He picked up his glass and drained the contents.

'It's an experience that I wouldn't like

to go through again,' he said, with a little shiver.

'Can you describe the car?' said the detective.

'Yes. It was a Spange,' answered the judge. 'An old make and painted blue.'

'Number?' said the detective, but Mr. Mallin shook his head.

'I never saw that,' he replied. 'I was too concerned in getting away to look.'

There was a fairly long pause during which Blackmore looked at his plate with a thoughtful frown.

How had these people known that the judge was going out to post his letters? It almost looked as though a close watch was being kept on the house, or — with a little start he remembered that softly closing door in the night — or had someone within Hillbrow given the information?

The car though, seemed to indicate that the whole episode had been carefully planned, or had it been kept somewhere close at hand in readiness in case a chance of getting himself or the judge presented itself?

That appeared most likely, but it only went to show the extraordinary thoroughness of these people.

'I should like to know just what Mr. Charles Evans and Mr. Basil Stacey were doing at the time you were attacked,' remarked Blackmore, breaking the long silence.

'It wasn't either of them who were in the car,' said the judge.

'Ah — no.' The detective nodded. 'You said that you saw the face of the man who was speaking to the driver. Did you recognise him?'

'Yes!' Mr. Mallin was barely audible and he moistened his dry lips. 'Yes, I recognised him.'

'Who was it?' John Blackmore leaned forward and his eyes gleamed.

'It was Simon Boyle!' said the judge, and his voice was the voice of a man who has seen a ghost!

17

The Man on the Tree

Up to this time the possibility of there being in existence an organisation that had taken upon itself the avenging of Simon Boyle was more or less a legend.

The Chief Commissioner at Scotland Yard refused to listen to Kenton's arguments, and frankly pooh-poohed the idea.

'Organised revenge is unknown to this country,' he said, impatiently. 'Besides, who could these people you speak of be? Boyle worked with no one and he had no gang. He may have had one or two agents, cheap little people like 'Harry the Dip' who were just paid workmen. They did what they were told and got paid for doing it, and after that they forgot they ever had anything to do with Boyle. You've been listening too much to Blackmore, Inspector, and he's prejudiced your outlook. He's a clever fellow but he's got too much imagination. He's never satisfied with simple explanations, and in spite of the sensational novels crime is simple, crooks are simple. That's why we catch 'em so easily.'

Kenton listened to this miniature lecture in silence. Then he went back to his own office with his opinion unaltered.

Later in the same day Blackmore had an interview with Colonel Baird and the result was to make the Chief Commissioner less sceptical.

'There may be something in it after all,' he admitted grudgingly, when the detective had outlined the whole series of events that had taken place after Boyle's execution. 'And I must say that if anything happens to Mallin I shall be convinced.'

John Blackmore raised his eyebrows.

'Am I to understand that the Judge must die in order to bring conviction to Scotland Yard?' he said icily, and the Commissioner's florid face went purple.

'Of course not!' he snapped. 'Don't be so ridiculous, Blackmore! What I meant was that if he were killed it would turn a possibility into a certainty.'

'So far as I am concerned no more proof is required,' retorted the detective.

Colonel Baird frowned and played with the pen-holder on his blotting pad.

'You may be perfectly satisfied,' he said, 'and I'll go as far as to say that after what you've told me I think that you are right. But we've got to go very carefully in the matter. There's not a shadow of evidence to connect the Evans' with the business, and if we take any steps and they turn nasty there'll be the very devil to pay. They could make it very unpleasant for us, and they'd have every newspaper and the entire population on their side.'

'The only steps I'm asking you to take are these,' said John Blackmore, and leaning forward he talked, and he talked to such purpose that that afternoon two strange men took up their positions at the drive gate of the Evans' house and occupied their time between leisurely breaking a heap of stones that had been disgorged there by the cart that had brought them, and watching the entrance and departure of every one who called on the occupants.

Mrs. Evans, on her way to pay a visit to Mr. Basil Stacey, saw them and a hard little smile curved her thin lips, for she had no illusions as to the reason for their presence.

Before returning to Hillbrow, where he had left Cartwright on guard, John Blackmore spent an unprofitable two hours at Somerset House. Unprofitable, because he failed to find among the long list of Evans' any with the Christian name of Charles that he could connect up with the people he suspected. Neither did the Staceys yield any better results, though he noted six families of that not uncommon name that would bear further investigations.

It was getting on for seven o'clock when he reached Esher. Nothing had happened during his absence and he was not surprised. He did not expect anything to happen during the daylight. It was at night that the blow would fall. The judge had extended his invitation to Cartwright, and the secretary, acting under his employer's orders, had accepted and had been allotted a bedroom next door to

Blackmore's, and they had arranged to take it in turn to watch, Blackmore from midnight ·to three, and Cartwright from thence until dawn.

The judge seemed rather depressed during the evening, and at dinner spoke little. Over coffee Blackmore confided his suspicions concerning the Evans' to him and he listened with growing amazement. 'I can't believe it possible,' he declared, shaking his grey head. 'Of course, I know nothing of their private affairs, but I have been friendly with them for — let me see — ' He wrinkled his forehead. ' — It must be nearly three years now. They have come over and dined about once a month, and I have gone over and played bridge with them. It's impossible that they could be concerned in any plot against me. Besides, they didn't even know Simon Boyle or Andrew Wilton, as he called himself. We've often mentioned him, wondering what he did with himself, for he seldom left his house. It's incredible to suppose that the Evans' had anything to do with him.'

'How long have they been living at their

present house?' asked John Blackmore, without going into an argument regarding the incredibility or otherwise of his belief.

'Over five years,' answered Mr. Justice Mallin. 'They've been here from — yes — about five years and a few months.'

'Simon Boyle took his house six years ago,' murmured the detective, and the conversation drifted into other channels.

Mr. Mallin excused himself after the meal on the plea that he had work to do and retired to his study, and Blackmore and his secretary filled in the evening playing chess.

It was early when the judge came in and wished them good night — barely eleven, and very shortly after they finished the game and also went to their rooms.

Nothing disturbed the peace of the night, and the dawn broke fresh and sweet smelling. It was a lovely morning with the first rays of the sun dispelling the mist, and Blackmore, who was feeling particularly wakeful, strolled into Cartwright's room a little after five, and finding the secretary just concluding his watch suggested a walk.

Cartwright accepted the suggestion with alacrity, and they crept down the stairs of the sleeping house and let themselves out by the side door.

The countryside lay bathed in a blue grey mist through which the golden light of the morning sun struggled to shine, and there was a stillness — the hush of the waking day that was somehow very pleasant.

Crossing the lawn they strolled through the narrow belt of trees by the shrubbery where Cartwright had kept his watch, and climbed the fence into the lane beyond.

'That looks rather enticing,' said Blackmore, pointing to a meadow of waving grass on his left.

They negotiated the five barred gate and went on, walking ankle deep in the emerald grass.

'We are probably trespassing,' the detective remarked, 'but I don't suppose there will be anybody about at this hour to stop us.'

'That's rather dangerous,' said Cartwright, pointing to a clump of trees ahead.

'Whoever owns this field ought to cut that down.'

Looking in the direction his secretary had indicated Blackmore saw the broken, hanging branch that had attracted his attention. It was swinging gently back and forth in the light breeze.

'It would be dangerous if it were anywhere else,' he said. 'But no one is likely to pass under it where it is. We've no right here and there's no sign of a footpath.'

They continued their walk, strolling in the direction of the clump of trees. The song of a lark broke out in the blue over-head and Cartwright was trying to catch a glimpse of the songster when he heard a sudden exclamation from Blackmore.

'What is it?' he began, but the detective had quickened his pace and was almost running towards the trees.

Cartwright caught up with him, and then he saw what it was that had caused that sudden startled ejaculation. The hanging thing that swayed from the tree was not a broken branch but the body of a man!

'Give me your knife, quick!' snapped Blackmore, and hauling himself up onto an overhanging branch he cut the rope that supported the ghastly object.

Cartwright caught it as it fell and laid it down on the long grass.

'Who is it?' he whispered huskily. His face was the colour of chalk for the dead man was not a pleasant sight.

'It *was* Jellis,' replied Blackmore, and his voice was hard. 'The public executioner and the man who hanged Simon Boyle!'

18

At a Dead End

John Blackmore turned from the twisted thing on the grass.

'Go back to the house,' he said sharply, 'and get through on the phone to the police station. Tell the inspector what's happened and ask him to come along at once!'

Cartwright nodded and hurried away, and after he had gone Blackmore knelt down beside the body and made a quick search of the pockets. He found nothing! Evidently the people who had been responsible for his death had robbed Jellis of whatever the man had had on him.

The detective frowned. How had the hangman been decoyed to this spot? Between hanging the executioner followed the calling of shoe repairer. He had a little shop in Hanley and only came away from his business on such occasions as the state demanded his services. He was a man of low mentality and sometimes drank more than was good for him, otherwise he was a respectable citizen, unmarried, who lived with and kept his invalid mother. There had been no execution lately that could have brought him away from his tiny shop. How then had he been enticed to Esher? By the same means as Fletcher the foreman of the jury? Probably, but they hadn't succeeded in discovering that yet.

Blackmore looked at the puffy swollen face of the dead man, and shook his head. James Lane, Fletcher, Jellis. Three people sacrificed to the memory of Simon Boyle. There only remained the judge now and himself. Blackmore smiled a little grimly. Evidently his presence at Hillbrow had upset their plans. They had intended to get Mr. Justice Mallin first and then Jellis. That was the correct order of things, but they had had to put off their attack on the judge and turn their attention to the poor little hangman — probably had planned his death in advance for that particular date.

Blackmore rose to his feet and made a search round the foot of the tree. The ground, however, was hard and there were no traces, and further afield it was useless looking, for the long grass showed nothing.

The detective was still prowling about, however, in the vague hope that he might come on something that would connect the Evans' with this latest tragedy when the police arrived in the form of an inspector and a constable and the divisional surgeon, who, from his sketchy attire, had evidently been dragged hastily from his bed.

Blackmore explained briefly to the horrified inspector how they had found the body, and waited to hear the doctor's verdict. His opinion was that death had been the result of strangulation. The vertebræ of the neck were intact, and from this the doctor concluded that the man had been dead before he had been hanged to the branch of the tree. As regards the time he had met his death so far as he could tell it must have been somewhere round about midnight.

The detective left the inspector to attend to the remaining details and accompanied by Cartwright walked back to Hillbrow and got out his car.

Half an hour's drive brought him to the Evans' house. The road menders were cooking some breakfast over a coke fire beside the heap of stones, and Blackmore stopped the car and approached them.

'Are you the men who have been on duty all night?' he asked, after he had made known his identity.

They replied in the affirmative. Their relief was expected in about an hour.

Blackmore told them of the finding of Jellis, but in reply to his further questions they shook their heads.

Nobody had gone in or come out of the house they were watching after eight o'clock on the previous night. If any of the occupants had left they must have gone by some other way than that of the drive.

This was the weak spot in the system of espionage that he had suggested. It was impossible, without employing a battalion, to keep a check on every way out of the grounds of the place, and the Chief Commissioner had refused point-blank to allow his men to be stationed any closer than the roadway.

In this he was acting sensibly as Blackmore had to admit, for there was no direct evidence against the Evans', and they could have claimed serious damages if the police had been found trespassing on their property.

He drove along the road by which they had come and turned off into a secondary road that led to the bungalow occupied by Mr. Basil Stacey. Although it was called a bungalow it was really a diminutive mansion, for it was built in the Tudor style and the garden that surrounded it was ablaze with flowers and garnished by curious examples of the topiary art. A few yards from the gate a man was sitting on a grassy bank, a bicycle by his side.

To him Blackmore put the same questions as he had asked the other detectives, and received almost the same answers. Mr. Basil Stacey had been out during the afternoon, had returned at half-past three, and shortly after Mr. and Mrs. Evans had called. They had remained until five and had then left. Mr. Stacey had pottered about in his garden during the evening, and until nearly midnight had sat on his lawn smoking and listening to the music supplied by the portable wireless. He had then gone in, locked up and turned out the lights, and had not yet appeared again.

Here again there was no means of telling whether or no Stacey had not found another means of leaving his little domain. In fact, the watchers, under their present restrictions, were practically useless as a means of checking the comings and goings of the people Blackmore suspected.

In a rather irritable mood the detective drove back to Hillbrow. The household was awake and the judge had been informed of the tragedy that had occurred during the night. It had apparently had a bad effect on him for he had gone back to his room with a sedative hastily prescribed by the divisional surgeon.

At half-past ten Inspector Kenton

arrived, hot, dusty, and bad tempered. He issued a lot of orders, scratched his head, and glared at everyone within the radius of his vision. Then he went off to consult John Blackmore.

He listened gloomily to all the detective had to say, pulling savagely at his moustache.

'This is bound to get into the papers,' he growled, 'can't keep it out. And then some fool reporter will link up the other crimes and there'll be a general how d'you do and outcry against the police.'

'I should think it was more than likely,' agreed Blackmore callously.

'Well, what can we do?' demanded the Scotland Yard man.

'I've done all I can,' said the detective. 'I've tried to get the Chief Commissioner have these people properly watched, and the result has been that he has sent three men down who might just as well have remained in London for all the good they've done. What is the use of keeping an eye on the drive gates of the Evans' house or the front of Stacey's bungalow. There are a hundred other ways they would use if they wanted to. They're not fools, they're perfectly aware of the reason for those men being where they are, and they are probably chuckling over the utter futility of the whole scheme.'

'I don't see what more we could do,' grunted Kenton. 'You see we've got to be careful — '

John Blackmore interrupted him with an impatient gesture.

'Careful!' he snapped. 'Yes, you've been careful enough. You've been so busy worrying about whether you were over-stepping the regulations that you have let an unfortunate man be killed. Poor Jellis is a victim of red tape if ever there was one!'

Kenton's red face went purple.

'Well, it isn't my fault!' he protested. 'I can't help it. I've got to obey orders!'

'I'm not blaming you personally,' said Blackmore, in a milder tone, 'or the Commissioner. I'm blaming the whole system.'

'You must admit, Blackmore,' said Kenton, 'that we've got absolutely nothing against these people beyond your own suspicions. There's nothing whatever to connect them with Simon Boyle or any of the murders, and you may be wrong.'

'I may be, but I'm not,' replied the detective. 'I'm perfectly willing to admit that there's no evidence against the Evans' or Stacey. On the other hand unless we can catch them red-handed, so to speak, neither is there ever likely to be. I doubt if even a search of their respective houses would lead to anything. They are much too clever. And anyway, a search warrant would never be granted.'

'We've struck a dead end,' said Kenton pessimistically, and left to interview the local inspector.

After lunch Blackmore went for a walk. He wanted to think, and he felt the gentle exercise would stimulate his brain. He strolled along the tree shaded road and unconsciously he took the direction that led to Mr. Stacey's bungalow. Mentally he went over every detail of the case trying to find a new lead, and he was almost startled when the hush of the afternoon was broken by the sound of footsteps. He looked up and saw a cool vision in white coming towards him and recognised the pale faced girl, Sonia. He raised his hat as she passed him and she smiled.

He must have gone on for nearly a hundred yards when he heard the swift pattering of feet behind him. Turning swiftly he saw that she was running back the way she had come.

'Mr. Blackmore!' she called breathlessly, and he stopped and waited.

She came up with him and laid her hand on his arm. She looked scared and frightened and her first words were startling enough.

'Are you very fond of life?' she asked, and then, before he could reply, 'if you are, go away from here — go away from England at once!'

19

The Warning

John Blackmore stared at the girl, and he saw by her expression the earnestness of her appeal. He also saw something else, she was not the same girl who had dined at Hillbrow a few nights ago. Her face was harder and paler and she looked as though she hadn't slept. Her dark eyes held a look of terror in their depths, and she kept on glancing quickly from side to side as if fearful that she might be seen.

'Exactly what do you mean?' he said quietly.

'Haven't I put it clearly enough?' Her breast was rising and falling rapidly, and what little colour she had ever possessed had gone from her cheeks, leaving them quite bloodless. 'Can't you understand plain English?' Her voice trembled and it was with an effort that she kept it under control.

Blackmore stood squarely before her,

his hands in his jacket pocket, his head bent a little, for she was much shorter than he.

'I can understand that you want me to leave England,' he answered. 'But I want to know why?'

'I'll tell you why,' she said impatiently. 'Listen! I hate you, John Blackmore. You don't know how I hate you! But I don't want you dead. Do you understand that? I don't want you dead!'

She didn't raise her voice but he didn't question the truth of her words. Her hate blazed from her dark eyes and was written in the straight line of her lips.

'I want you to live,' she went on, rapidly, huskily. 'I'm tired of death. Sick of it! The smell of blood is in my nostrils all the time!' She flung out her arms wildly and the detective thought she was going to break into hysterics, but she checked her emotion. 'There's no reason why I want you to live except that I'm tired of dead men and their ghosts!' She screwed up her eyes tight with an expression of intense anguish. 'Will you get out of this case — go away and leave them to it — all of them?'

'Leave who to it?' he asked quickly. 'Whom are you speaking about?'

'I can't tell you that, you know I can't tell you,' she answered. 'But if you don't get out they'll get you. Go abroad for four months — two months or even one month would be long enough!'

'Who are the people you are warning me against?' he repeated, and she jerked her head impatiently.

'I'm not going to tell you,' she said. 'You know — without.'

'The Evans'?' He looked down at her steadily.

'I'm not going to tell you,' she cried again. 'Not because I'm afraid of what you would do to me. I'd be glad if you'd arrest me here and now and keep me locked up until it's all over — everything.' She grasped his arm. 'Won't you do what I ask?' she pleaded. 'Won't you give it up and go away?'

He shook his head.

'No, Miss Evans, I won't,' he said. 'I appreciate your warning but I'm not going to run away.'

She made a gesture of despair.

'You don't know what you're up against,' she muttered.

Blackmore laughed.

'That's where you're wrong,' he answered. 'I'm quite aware what I am up against, but I'm not going to give in. I'm not going to rest until I've put the people who killed 'Harry the Dip,' James Lane, Fletcher and poor Jellis on the trap where Simon Boyle stood!'

She flushed and recoiled as if he had struck her.

'You'll never do it,' she said huskily. 'They'll have you first.'

'I shall do it,' said the detective sternly. 'Answer me this, Miss Evans. Who was Simon Boyle?'

'Who was Simon Boyle?' She laughed, a harsh, mirthless sound that grated. 'Oh, you don't know that then? I'll tell you who Simon Boyle was. He was a myth, a nobody, a ghost!'

'Look here, Miss Evans,' he took her arm gently. 'You've said too much and you've said too little. Why don't you tell me everything?'

'You know why,' she answered. 'I'd never have said so much only I'm afraid of two things. I'm afraid of them killing you and I'm afraid of them failing. Because if they fail the next time you'll have them, and that will be the end of everything!'

She gave a startled gasp as there came the sound of footsteps along the road, and then, before Blackmore could stop her she turned and ran away like a frightened rabbit. Almost before she had disappeared round the bend the newcomer hove in sight. A slim youthful figure in the newest of grey flannel suits. It was Basil Stacey. He greeted Blackmore with an expansive smile.

'Perfectly lovely afternoon — what?' he remarked. 'Nothing like the English countryside on a summer's day. By Jove, no!'

'Taking your constitutional, Mr. Stacey?' asked Blackmore blandly.

'Yes, doctor's orders,' replied the immaculate youth. 'Deuced fag and all that, but got to do it. Helps to keep the jolly old fat down, y'know.'

He passed on with a cheery nod and

the detective watched him until he too had passed round the curve in the road and then he continued to walk, and he had much to think about.

Sonia Evans' warning had, so far as he was concerned, confirmed his suspicions. The Evans' were at the back of the business. Now how was it possible to get definite evidence against them? Even if he repeated word for word what the pale-faced girl had told him, in a witness box, it wouldn't cut any ice unless she substantiated it, and of course it wasn't likely she would do that. It must have taken all her courage to have stopped and spoken as she had done.

Blackmore felt sorry for her, she looked terribly ill. The strain was playing havoc with her nerves, and she had, of course, been forced into the affair through her parents. If only he could have got her to talk more. A word from her and all his difficulties would be smoothed out, and she was practically at the end of her tether. It would not take much to make her speak and give the whole business away. It was really worth trying to seek another interview.

It seemed a pretty awful thing to try and persuade a daughter to give her own mother and father away, but these people were scarcely human. After all, it was considerably worse to take human life, and they had been guilty of three murders. There seemed to be a streak of decency in the girl's nature that was worth fostering, and if she were taken away from her parents' influence and put among different surroundings that streak would have a chance to ascend itself.

Blackmore turned the matter over in his mind as he strolled along and he decided that he would, at the first opportunity, have another talk with Sonia Evans. But the opportunity was not to present itself.

Blackmore and Cartwright were sitting at dinner that night, the only two at the long polished table, for the judge had not left his room all day and had sent a message excusing himself, when young Harry Morris came in, looking rather white and strained. He apologised for being late, and he looked so ill as he hurriedly took his place that Blackmore asked him what was the matter.

'I'm rather worried,' he said. 'Of course you haven't heard. Sonia — er — Miss Evans has been taken seriously ill, and had to be sent away to a nursing home.'

The detective's eyes narrowed.

'When was this?' he asked sharply.

'This afternoon,' replied the secretary. 'She'd been out for a walk and was taken ill immediately she got back home.'

'And they've taken her to a nursing home, have they?'

Morris nodded gloomily.

'Yes, she left in the car an hour ago.'

'Did they tell you which nursing home she'd been taken to?' inquired Blackmore.

'No, somewhere by the coast I think. She's got to have plenty of sunshine and sea air. I only wish I did know where she was,' burst out the secretary.

John Blackmore made no comment but he was very doubtful if Sonia Evans was anywhere near the sea, or in a position to get much sunshine. Evidently someone had seen her interview with him that afternoon, and had taken the precaution to ensure that it wasn't repeated. He wasn't afraid that the girl had suffered any physical harm. They had just removed her for the time being to some place where she couldn't talk, and couldn't be found. The detective gave a little involuntary shiver. These people were so thorough that for an instant they had almost succeeded in making him feel scared!

20

Lightning Sam Strikes Lucky

On an evening two days later Mr. Samuel Robins came out of the little coffee shop in Westminster Bridge Road and turned his shuffling steps towards the glittering lights of the West End.

He was a little, shabby, furtive man, with an unhealthy complexion, and under his cap his hair was cut close to his head. It was not Mr. Robins' pleasure that he wore his hair in this fashion. His own inclination favoured it rather longer, well oiled and brushed into a quiff on his forehead. But at Wandsworth Prison where he had spent a considerable part of that year they were rather arbitrary in the matter of hair-dressing and had views of their own.

Mr. Robins was a pick-pocket, although he refused to admit this in his own circle of friends, preferring to call himself a 'bank smasher,' although it was doubtful if he had ever entered a bank in his life, either legitimately or otherwise, and it is certain that even if he had been turned loose in the strong room with a kit of the latest burglar's tools the contents of the safe would have remained intact, for he knew nothing about locks having once tried vainly to let himself into his own lodgings with a piece of bent wire on an occasion when he had forgotten his key.

But Mr. Robins had his pride, and liked to imagine that his friends on reading the account of the smashing of the Counties and Central Bank, would smile to themselves and say in admiring voices: 'I wonder if this is 'Lightning Sam's' work?'

Not that they ever did, for Mr. Robins' friends were perfectly aware that he was incapable of breaking into a hen coop, but it gave him a certain amount of satisfaction to think so, and even a little pick-pocket is entitled to his vanities.

This evening he was on business bent. In a quarter of an hour all the theatres would be disgorging their crowds of pleasure seekers, and Mr. Robins hoped to be able to pick up something really worth having. It was urgently necessary that he should, for after paying for his supper of bread and butter and coffee he possessed the not very large sum of fourpence, and although Mr. Robins had not by any means expensive tastes he did not consider that fourpence was a sum compatible to the station of a 'bank smasher.'

Passing over Westminster Bridge he walked up Whitehall and presently found himself at Leicester Square Tube Station. Here he halted and looked about him, trying to make up his mind whether he should try Shaftesbury Avenue or Coventry Street, both favourite hunting grounds of his. He decided on Coventry Street and crossed the road.

It was that hour when, for a moment, London seems to rest. The traffic is at a low ebb, for the taxis are grouped round the theatres, and the private cars were parked in the squares and side streets, waiting for the time to emerge and pick up their owners.

Mr. Robins was shuffling past the blazing vestibule of Daly's theatre when a long bonneted black saloon glided into the kerb just before him and stopped.

'Get in!' said a voice.

'Lightning Sam' looked round. He never for a moment dreamed that the voice was addressing him, but the pavement round him at that moment was deserted and he was curious to see to whom the invitation had been extended.

'I mean you — Robins — quick. Get in!'

Mr. Robins stopped in sheer amazement. There was no doubt about it. The owner of the black saloon whose face was hidden in the darkness within was calling him.

He came over to the car.

'You speakin' to me, Guv'nor?' he whined.

For answer the polished door was jerked open.

'Yes, you fool,' grated an impatient voice. 'Don't stand there attracting attention. Get in!'

Mr. Robins hesitated, all the habitual

suspicion of his kind aroused.

'What for?' he demanded not unreasonably.

'I want you to do a little job. There'll be a hundred in it for you. Fifty pounds now and another fifty when you've carried it out,' said the stranger.

Mr. Robins remembered the fourpence in his pocket, and his hesitation disappeared. He got into the car with alacrity. The unknown made room for him by his side and tapped on the window.

Smoothly the car drew away from the kerb and headed towards Piccadilly.

'What yer want done?' asked Mr. Robins, hoarsely, and pinched himself to make sure that this strange adventure was not a dream.

'I want a man's pocket picked,' said the owner of the car, continuing, 'you are a pick-pocket, aren't you?'

'In me spare time, Guv'nor,' said Mr. Robins, remembering his reputation. 'When I ain't engaged on anything bigger.' He tried to catch a glimpse of the other's face in the flashing lights that splashed through the saloon's windows, but in this he was disappointed, for the man wore a handkerchief which was tied round his nose and mouth. 'Whose pocket d'yer want 'dipped'?' he added.

There was a momentary silence.

'Do you know Fryman?' enquired the masked man suddenly.

'Can't say as I do,' replied Sam, scratching his head. ''Oo's 'e?'

The man clicked his teeth impatiently.

'I thought everybody knew Walter Fryman,' he muttered. 'You can't pick up a paper without seeing his name. Still, if you don't know — he's a millionaire several times over. He's a German by birth and an Englishman by naturalisation, and he lives in a block of flats in Park Lane.'

'Does 'e?' said Mr. Robins, whose conversational powers were not very well developed.

'Every evening at eight o'clock he dines in the restaurant attached to the block, and at nine he walks to his club in Piccadilly,' said the owner of the car. 'I should think that would be the best time for you to — er — operate.'

''Ow will I know 'im?' asked Mr. Robins.

'I will point him out to you,' said the man. 'He carries a wallet in his inside breast pocket — that's what I want.'

Mr. Robins looked at the man beside him curiously.

'What d'yer want 'is wallet for, Guv'nor?' he said. ''E don't carry 'is millions abart with 'im, does 'e?'

'No, you fool,' snarled the other sharply. 'And it's no business of yours what I want the wallet for. I'm offering you a hundred pounds to get it for me, and that's all that concerns you.'

'Awlright, keep yer 'air on,' said 'Lightning Sam.' 'If that's all yer want it's as easy as kiss yer 'and.'

'You'll do it?'

'For an 'undred of the best?' Mr. Robins' voice was jubilant, 'I'd pick the pocket of the 'Ome Secretary fer a 'undred quid!'

'Good! Then be outside the picture theatre at Marble Arch, the new one, at ten minutes to nine to-morrow night,' said the stranger, 'and I'll pick you up.'

He leaned forward and tapped on the window. The car was running slowly along Piccadilly, and now it swung into a side street and pulled up. The man with the handkerchief round his face opened the door.

'Don't forget, ten to nine,' he said.

'Wait a minute,' said Mr. Robins. 'Don't be in such a bloomin' 'urry. What abart the fifty on account?'

'I'm sorry. I forgot.' The man felt in his pocket and produced a packet that rustled pleasurably. 'Here you are.' He thrust the packet into 'Lightning Sam's' willing palm. 'You shall have the other fifty when you've completed the job.'

Mr. Robins slipped the money into his ragged coat pocket and got out. He had scarcely reached the pavement before the door was slammed behind him and the car bounded forward with a jerk.

He watched the red tail lamp dwindling away and repeated to himself the number until it was fixed in his memory, but he needn't have taken the trouble, for Mr. Basil Stacey had only fixed the plate that evening and had every intention of removing it the moment he got back to his bungalow.

When the car was out of sight Mr. Robins turned and shuffled off towards Tottenham Court Road where he knew of a little club that welcomed people with fifty pounds in their possession.

By two o'clock he was very drunk and telling all his friends he had just come back from smashing the strong room at the Bank of England!

21

Before the Storm

The three days that elapsed following the discovery of Jellis's murder and the removal of Sonia Evans to a problematical nursing home were conspicuous only for their entire lack of incident.

Day succeeded day and there was no whisper from the enemy. Life at Hillbrow went on peacefully and quietly like the placid surface of a pond, and yet deep underneath the treacherous currents were eddying, invisibly preparing for the horrible climax. This sudden calm was abnormal and it made John Blackmore uneasy. Something was brewing and of that he felt certain, and he didn't know what it was. There was an oppressive expectancy in the atmosphere, like the hush before the lightning flash. And then, in the midst of the peace and quiet of the summer's evening the blow fell.

The day had been more than unusually hot, and Blackmore and Cartwright had spent most of it sprawling in deck chairs on the lawn. Mr. Justice Mallin had not as yet entirely recovered from the shock of Jellis's death, and they had seen very little of him.

The inquest had taken place that morning and the police had asked for and been granted an adjournment, so the proceedings had been of the briefest. From Blackmore's point of view the whole thing was very unsatisfactory. He knew the people responsible and could do nothing. His hands were completely tied for lack of proof. Unless they made a false move that would bring them out into the open he was helpless, and he hated inaction.

Scheme after scheme had been evolved in his keen brain, only to be rejected as useless when he had fully analysed them. That they would make some move eventually against the judge he was sure, and in that lay his one hope. The thing that puzzled him most was who was at the back of the Evans'? He was convinced that both they and Stacey were only tools, wielded by someone unknown. Was this directing genius the man who had attacked him at Simon Boyle's house and who was the living image of the dead forger? And if so, who was he?

Blackmore shifted irritably in his chair and flung away the butt of the cigar he had been smoking. He had thought round again in a vicious circle. The beginning and the end of this wretched business rested in the answer to one question. Who had Simon Boyle been? And here was a blank wall, rigid and unpenetrable, against which he battered his head in vain.

Cartwright raised his eyes from the book he had been attempting to read at the sudden creaking of the detective's chair.

'What's the matter?' he asked. 'Got the hump?'

'Something very near it,' replied Blackmore.

'Come for a walk?'

The detective shook his head.

'Can't,' he said. 'I'm expecting a phone

call from Kenton. He's been up to Hanley to interview Jellis's mother with the object of finding out, if possible, what brought the man away from his business. He'll be back this evening and he promised to let me know the result — if any.'

The secretary laid aside his book and rose to his feet, stretching himself with a yawn.

'I think I'll take a stroll round,' he remarked.

'All right,' said the detective. 'Cut along.'

Cartwright sauntered off down the drive. It was a lovely evening and comparatively cool after the heat of the day. Reaching the gates he paused in the roadway deciding which direction to take. To the left the road led down into Esher, and to the right there was a shady lane that wound its way through the wood and then came out into open country.

He chose the right and as he turned and strolled up the white road to the entrance of the narrow lane, a man who had been lying along a branch of a tall tree some two hundred yards away and watching the drive gates of Hillbrow through a pair of field glasses, smiled to himself and descended from his precarious perch.

The secretary went on, completely unconscious of the figure that was hurrying across two intervening fields to a gate that would eventually bring it out into the very lane that Cartwright was traversing and some few yards ahead of him.

Turning a bend in the winding track Harry saw a man approaching but took no notice of him until the stranger drew almost level with him, and then he was about to pass when the man stopped.

'Excuse me,' he said in a rough voice, 'but could yer tell me if I'm right fcr Esher?'

'Yes.' Harry turned and pointed along the way he had come. 'Keep straight along until you get to — '

Something crashed down with stunning force on his head, and the remainder of the sentence ended in a gasping cry — the countryside split into a thousand flashes of stabbing lights and then everything went black as he fell backwards into his assailant's arms!

The man lowered him to the ground, glanced swiftly about him and then, taking a small case from the pocket of his ragged coat, extracted a hypodermic syringe, and pushing the needle into the secretary's arm, pressed home the plunger. Replacing syringe and case in his pocket he stooped, and picking up the secretary he carried him to the side of the lane and dropped him among some thick bushes that grew there.

As soon as he had made certain that he was completely concealed from view the man left him and hurried across the fields the way he had come.

The tree from which he had been watching was one of a small copse that stood near the edge of the secondary road that led to Basil Stacey's bungalow, and in a field by this copse was a dilapidated and long disused barn. As a matter of fact it was part of Mr. Justice Mallin's estate, and the judge had many times considered the advisability of having the rotting structure pulled down. At the present time, however, it was serving an unusual purpose, for the man who had struck Cartwright down opened the door, disappeared within the gloomy interior, and presently re-appeared driving an ancient saloon car.

Without troubling to shut the barn door — it only hung by one rusty hinge — he sent the car bumping over the uneven surface of the field, stopped to open a gate, and brought the machine into the road. A quarter of an hour later he was back at the place where he had hidden the young man, and picking him up he bundled him inside the car, locked the doors, and once more resuming his place at the wheel, turned round.

He achieved this with difficulty for the lane was narrow, but eventually he succeeded, and presently was driving along the main road as fast as the ancient car would take him.

Cartwright was recovering consciousness when the car stopped. He felt dull and heavy, there was an unpleasant taste in his mouth and his head ached horribly.

He was dimly aware that someone was dragging him along over uneven ground, and then he was flung roughly on a hard floor, that felt gritty and smelt of new wood. He opened his eyes and saw a patch of fading daylight coming through a square curtainless window, and then stared up at the man who was standing over him, surveying him dispassionately.

'Where — am — I?' he asked dully, sitting up and clasping his splitting head between his hands.

His brain was whirling, he couldn't think clearly and a thousand knives seemed to be stabbing through the top of his skull.

'Here — drink this,' said a voice. The man took a flask from his pocket and unscrewing the top poured out some golden fluid into the cuplike stopper.

'It's only brandy, you fool. You needn't be scared,' he snarled as Harry feebly tried to push it away.

He forced the scorching liquor between his teeth, the spirit was choking but it revived him a little.

'What am I doing here?' he asked thickly.

'You're here because I brought you here,' retorted the other, 'and you're miles away from anywhere so if you start screaming you'll only waste your breath.'

Cartwright looked about him wonderingly. He was in a square bare room, the walls of which were not even papered, the floor of brand new wood. There was no furniture of any kind, and the place reeked with the smell of paint. He felt too ill even to think. His limbs felt as heavy as lead and all he wanted to do was to sleep. He tried to put up a feeble resistance when the man brought some rope and began to tie his ankles and wrists, but everything was spinning round and his attempts were useless.

'You can stop like that until your cursed employer joins you,' were the last words he heard before the drug that flooded his system once more asserted itself and everything faded to nothingness!

22

The House of Death

Dusk had faded into darkness before Blackmore began to feel anxious, but when ten o'clock struck and there was no sign of his secretary he felt more than a twinge of uneasiness. What could have happened to him? It had been a little before eight when he had started out for his stroll. Certainly two hours was not long if he had gone for any sort of a walk, but he had only given Blackmore the impression that he was going for a short stroll.

By eleven he was seriously alarmed, and he had just decided to go out and see if he could see anything of him when Cramp came to inform him that he was wanted on the telephone. The instrument was in the judge's study, and thinking it was the call he had been expecting from Kenton he hurried to answer the summons, his mind still occupied with the whereabouts of Cartwright. But when he picked up the receiver it was a strange voice that came to him over the wire.

'That Mr. John Blackmore?' it enquired gruffly.

'Yes,' replied the detective. 'Who is that speaking?'

'Police Constable Raven, sir,' was the reply. 'I'm afraid I've got bad news for you. Your secretary Cartwright has been knocked down by a car on the arterial road!'

Blackmore was startled.

'Is he — badly hurt?' he asked, in concern.

'Yes, sir, I'm sorry to say he is,' went on the gruff voice. 'The accident happened near where they are building some new houses, sir, and we've taken 'im into the first one. He's asking for you, sir, and the doctor says it's only a question of minutes. The car caught him in the back, injured his spine!'

'I'll be there at once. How do I find the place?'

The man at the other end gave him instructions, and slamming up the receiver he almost ran out of the study.

'My secretary — met with an accident,' he rasped sharply to Cramp as he flew across the hall, and the next second he was racing round to the garage.

In under two minutes from the time of leaving the study he had got out the car and was driving it at a reckless speed down the drive. Scarcely slackening he swerved out of the gates and went speeding up the road, and he kept up that mad rush until he reached his destination.

He couldn't miss the place to which Cartwright had been taken. It stood by itself half way along the new arterial road, a solitary red brick house, glaringly new, surrounded by the litter that builders leave behind and call a garden, and with a shrieking of brakes Blackmore brought the car to a standstill. As he leaped down from the driving seat a dim figure came out of the shadow of the doorway.

'You Mr. Blackmore?' it said, and when the detective answered hurriedly in the affirmative: 'the doctor and the policeman are inside with your secretary. He's in the room on the right.'

Blackmore pushed past him and threw open the door he had indicated.

'Am I in time?' he said, and stopped dead on the threshold, staring at the yellow-faced woman who was smiling mockingly at him in the light of a candle.

'In plenty of time, Mr. Blackmore,' she said. 'In fact the person you have been asked to meet has not yet arrived.'

John Blackmore looked round the empty room, and his first sensation was one of relief that the thing he had expected was not true.

'So it was a trap, eh?' he remarked.

She nodded.

'Yes — rather ingenious, don't you think?' she laughed, and the corners of her thin mouth lifted in a sneer. 'You thought you were very clever, but we've won.'

The detective raised his eyebrows.

'At least you are running true to type,' he said coolly. 'All criminals suffer from an overwhelming vanity.'

'Vanity or not we've beaten you,' she retorted, and added sharply: 'don't move. Keep your hands still!'

Blackmore had moved his right hand towards his breast pocket and as he did so he felt the cold ring of a pistol barrel pressed against his neck from behind.

'Don't you try and start anything,' said the gruff voice of the man who had met him in the doorway. 'It'll be the worse for you if you do.'

Blackmore shrugged his shoulders.

'Really,' he remarked, 'you people are easily scared. I was merely going to take out my cigarette case.'

'You won't need any more cigarettes,' said the woman grimly, and slipping her hand into the pocket of the long coat she was wearing she brought out a small automatic.

'All right, Frank,' she said sharply. 'Tie him up.'

The muzzle of the pistol that was pressing into his neck was removed, and his arms were seized in a firm grip and jerked behind his back. There was the jangle of metal and he felt his wrists encircled by the cold clasp of handcuffs. They locked with a click.

'Quite professional,' he murmured

approvingly, and then the man stooped quickly and a second pair were secured about his ankles. As he rose he came into the light of the candle and Blackmore saw his face for the first time. It was the man who had attacked him in Simon Boyle's house.

'I thought it was you,' he said pleasantly. 'So your name's Frank, is it? What's your other name?'

'You mind your own business,' he snarled angrily.

'I am,' said Blackmore. 'My business is to enquire into everything that is in connection with criminals.'

'Get over in that corner and don't talk so much,' snapped Mrs. Evans, and the man called Frank gripped him by the arm and pushed him forward. The manacles on his ankles forced him to shuffle but there was sufficient length of chain to allow him to walk. Reaching the corner he leaned back against the wall. 'Go and take his car round to the back,' said the woman, and the man nodded and went out. Shortly after Blackmore heard the purr of the engine.

'May I ask what we are waiting for?' he enquired. 'I'm getting rather bored.'

Mrs. Evans glared at him malignantly. 'You'll see what we're waiting for soon,' she rasped. 'And then you'll have plenty to keep you amused.'

'Is the charming Mr. Evans coming, and the delightful Mr. Stacey?'

She nodded.

'Quite a family party,' said Blackmore. 'What a pity that Simon Boyle can't be here to complete it.'

Her lined yellow face twisted into such an expression of hatred as Blackmore had seldom seen before in a human being.

'So you know?' she grated between her teeth.

'I guessed,' replied the detective, 'but I couldn't prove it. What relation was Simon Boyle to you?'

'He was my husband,' she whispered the words almost inaudibly and Blackmore started.

He had not expected that. He had, as he said, guessed that the Evans' and Boyle were in some way related, but he had never dreamed of this relationship.

'Now do you understand why I hate you, John Blackmore?' she hissed. 'I hated all those who were responsible for Simon's death!'

'Who was Simon Boyle?' asked Blackmore, and she laughed.

'That you will know when James arrives,' she answered. 'Just before the end. It will be the last knowledge that you will carry to your grave!'

She stopped and listened. There was the sound of footsteps in the passage, and then the door opened and Charles Evans came in.

'So you've got him,' he said, as his eyes fell on the detective. 'Where's his secretary?'

'In the other room,' replied the woman.

Evans licked his lips, and Blackmore saw that his hands were trembling. 'What time is James coming?' he asked.

'He should be here at any moment now,' she replied.

He walked over and leaned against the mantelpiece, and removing his hat wiped his forehead with his handkerchief.

'I shall be glad when it's over,' he

muttered, and she flashed him a contemptuous glance.

'Are you going to be the Lord High Executioner?' asked Blackmore, and although he continued to speak lightly his heart was heavy for he knew that these people would show no mercy. They hated him with a hatred that only death could end. A hatred that after Mrs. Evans' admission he could understand.

Charles Evans shook his head.

'No, I'm not,' he said. 'That's nothing to do with me. I'm only here to put you where you won't be found after!'

Blackmore was feeling gingerly at the handcuffs about his wrists. Once an Indian Fakir had mystified him by the ease with which he was able to free himself from these manacles, and a handful of rupees had bought his secret. Now the detective was trying hard to compress the bones of his right hand as the Indian had taught him, but with a sinking of the heart he realised the truth of the man's words when he had said: 'You must practice every day for this trick or it can never be done.' Still fumbling at his wrists he looked steadily at Evans.

'What are you going to do with my secretary?'

Again the man shook his head.

'I don't know,' he replied. 'James has views about him. I don't know what they are. He knows too much about us to live.'

'He knows nothing,' said the detective. 'He doesn't know that your supposed wife is the widow of Simon Boyle. He doesn't know that Basil Stacey is her son. He doesn't know that you and Boyle were brothers. He doesn't even know who James is.'

'Do you?' muttered Evans quickly.

'Yes. I knew directly you called him James,' answered Blackmore.

'You seem to know a lot!' Evans' face was streaming with perspiration. 'How did you find it out?'

'Mrs. Evans told me of her relationship with Boyle,' said the detective. 'The other, I must admit, was guesswork. What is it to be, a hanging or a shooting?'

'I don't know,' growled Evans again, and Blackmore laughed.

'You seem strangely ignorant,' he said,

and looked round the bare, white-washed room. 'Know what this place reminds me of, Evans? It reminds me of the execution shed. It only wants the trap, the wooden beam, the release lever, and the steel winch ... It's a curious feeling to be wakened up at six o'clock on a grey morning and be told to dress in the clothes you wore at the trial! Ever read Wilde's poem:

'The hangman with his gardener's gloves
Slips through the padded door.
And binds one with three leather thongs
That the throat may thirst no more?'

'Curse you!' screamed Charles Evans, his face livid and his eyes wide with fear. 'Keep your mouth shut, can't you?'

'He's only trying to scare you, you fool,' said the yellow-faced woman, and the contempt in her voice was biting. 'And he seems to have succeeded. You oughtn't to be in this business at all!'

'I wish to Heaven I wasn't,' muttered

Evans. 'I wish I was well out of it.'

'Bah! You've got no nerve,' she said. 'Simon always said you were white-livered. How you ever came to be his brother I don't know.' She looked towards the window as from outside came the squeak of a car's brakes. 'There's James,' she said. 'Go and meet him, Charles.'

The man went out and Mrs. Evans turned her large eyes towards Blackmore.

'Now, Mr. John Blackmore,' she said venomously. 'You've got a very little while to live so you'd better make the most of it!'

John Blackmore said nothing. He was gazing at the door. Presently there came a dull murmur of voices and then the sound of a step. A second later a tall form appeared on the threshold.

'Come in James,' greeted Mrs. Evans, and Mr. Edward James Mallin entered the dimly lighted room!

23

The Letter

Mr. Samuel Robins rose late, and it cannot be said that he was feeling his best. He had been practically carried home on the previous night — or rather in the early hours of the morning — and his head felt at least three sizes too large for him. This state of affairs was not due to conceit but the result of the many drinks he had consumed at the club in Tottenham Court Road. He counted the remainder of his wealth and grunted disgustedly. Of the fifty pounds only twenty remained. Somebody must have been helping themselves freely while he was fuddled. He couldn't have spent such a big amount.

'Can't even trust yer friends,' said Mr. Robins bitterly. 'Thieves and vagabonds, that's what they are.'

He dressed leisurely, finding it difficult

to lace his boots on account of the trembling of his hands, and at four o'clock sallied forth to his favourite coffee shop.

A substantial meal made him feel a little better, although his head still ached vilely, and presently, at opening time he drifted into a public house and consumed a double brandy. He consumed several and by the time it was drawing near for his appointment at Marble Arch he was feeling so much better that it was with difficulty he prevented a desire to burst into song.

Punctual to the minute he arrived outside the picture house, and almost at the same instant the closed car drew into the kerb. Mr. Robins walked over to it with a slight swagger. He felt himself to be an important man. He was consorting with swell crooks, not mean little sneak thieves.

'Here we are,' he greeted as the door was opened. 'Always rely on Sam Robins. Never let you down.'

'Get in, you fool!' said the man inside. 'Do you want to attract attention?'

Mr. Robins got in and flopped beside his employer.

'Now then,' he said. 'Show me this bloke with the money and I'll do the job. Couldn't have found anyone better'n me to do it. There isn't anybody would do it s'well as me.'

Basil Stacey eyed him apprehensively.

'You've been drinking,' he snapped curtly.

'Lightning Sam' drew himself up with dignity.

'I've had a livener,' he said. 'A man's entitled to a livener isn't he when he's got a ticklish job ter do? Don't you worry abart me, Guv'nor, I'm all right.'

'You might have kept off the drink until this business was over,' retorted the other. 'I don't want it bungled.'

'I'm all right,' said Mr. Robins again, and Stacey leaned forward and tapped on the window. As he did so Sam caught sight of a corner of white projecting from his coat pocket.

It looked like a letter. Visions of converting the hundred pounds into several hundreds by a little judicious blackmail entered Mr. Robins' mind and when Stacey leaned back in his seat and the car moved forward the letter that had reposed in his pocket had passed into the possession of 'Lightning Sam.'

The car swung round into Park Lane, and the man who drove it had evidently received his instructions for opposite the vestibule of a restaurant that was attached to a huge block of flats he stopped the machine and getting down from his seat, lifted the radiator and began tinkering with the engine.

Mr. Stacey sat in silence, his eyes fixed on the revolving doors of the restaurant. Five minutes passed and then he sat forward sharply.

'That's the man!' he said quickly, and following the direction of his hand Mr. Robins saw a stout thick-set man in a blue suit come leisurely out.

He paused on the pavement, took a cigar case from his pocket, selected a cigar, bit off the end and lighted it. Then he turned and walked up Park Lane in the direction of Piccadilly.

'Go on,' snapped Basil Stacey. 'There's your man. I'll keep an eye on you from the car, and when you've got it I'll pick you up in a side street.'

'Right, Guv'nor!' said Mr. Robins, getting out. 'It won't take me a jiffy!'

He shuffled off in the wake of the millionaire, and when he had gone some two hundred yards the driver of the car resumed his seat and sent the machine following slowly behind him.

'Lightning Sam' decided to postpone his operations until his victim had reached the more crowded thoroughfare of Piccadilly, and occupied the intervening time by trying to still the trembling of his hands. But the amount of drink he had consumed had played havoc with his nerves and he found this very difficult. His unsuspecting quarry walked on, enjoying both the gentle exercise and the fragrant cigar, and presently turned out of Hamilton Place into Piccadilly. When he was strolling along opposite the Green Park, Mr. Robins decided that it was a favourable spot for the job.

He increased his pace, and choosing a moment when the millionaire was passing through a group of people coming in the other direction Mr. Robins stumbled up against him, clutching at him wildly to prevent himself from falling.

'I'm sorry, Guv'nor,' he muttered apologetically. 'Beg yer parden.'

The millionaire muttered something and 'Lightning Sam' hurried on, the wallet he had extracted from the other's pocket now reposing in his own.

'Easy,' said Mr. Robins to himself, and then gulped as a hand caught him by the arm and swung him round.

'At it again, Sam?' said a reproachful voice, and he looked up into the smiling face of a large man who was holding him in a painful grip.

'Watcher mean? I wasn't doin' nuthin',' whined Mr. Robins, struggling to free himself.

'Come, come, Sam,' said Detective-Inspector Kenton. 'It won't wash. It's a fair cop. I saw the whole thing. You're getting careless in your old age. What did you take out of that gentleman's pocket?'

'Nuthin',' began Sam, and then stopped as the millionaire drew level with them and Kenton spoke to him.

'Would you mind feeling in your pocket

and telling me if you've lost anything, sir,' he said.

Mr. Fryman halted and look startled.

'Lost anything?' he repeated, and then: 'Oh, this fellow who stumbled into me — you mean — ' He hurriedly ran through his pockets. 'My wallet!' he exclaimed, and 'Lightning Sam', with a sinking heart, gave up his protestations of innocence.

'All right,' he sighed. 'It's a fair cop!' He pulled the wallet from his pocket and held it out. 'I ain't 'ad nuthin' to eat fer five days,' he began dolefully, but Kenton cut him short.

'But you've had plenty to drink by the look of you,' he snapped. 'Come on, they'll give you a meal at Vine Street!'

Accompanied by the angry Mr. Fryman, Kenton deposited his prisoner in Vine Street, and 'Lightning Sam' was duly charged.

'A bloke in a car asked me to do it,' asserted Sam, 'and that's the truth. That's me own money you've got there,' he added, pointing to the contents of his pockets which had been piled on the desk in the charge room. 'I was to 'ave 'ad another fifty quid if I'd pulled the job off!'

'Is this letter yours, sir,' asked the station sergeant, looking at Mr. Fryman.

The millionaire glanced at the envelope.

'No,' he said, shaking his head. 'I don't know anybody called Basil Stacey.'

'What's that!' snapped Kenton sharply. 'Here, Sergeant, give me that letter!'

'I took it out of the feller's pocket what asked me ter do the job,' said Mr. Robins angrily. 'There y'are. That's proof I'm tellin' yer the truth.'

But Kenton wasn't listening. With a face that was suddenly pale he was reading the contents of the letter he had taken from the envelope.

'Great Heavens!' he exclaimed, and then: 'What's the time? Eleven thirty! Look after this fellow, Sergeant, I must get back to the Yard!' He darted out of the police station and hailed a taxi.

Twenty minutes later a long police car thundered away from the Embankment entrance of Scotland Yard packed with plain-clothes men. Kenton was seated beside the driver and his face was very grim and set!

24

The Executioner

Mr. Edward James Mallin stood in the doorway and surveyed the detective with a malignant smile twisting his thin lips.

'So you have fallen into the trap, Mr. Blackmore,' he sneered. 'Well, well, everything has turned out very nicely. The others have been disposed of — you — you who were the means of bringing my poor brother to his death — you are the last!'

John Blackmore looked at him contemptuously, but he remained silent.

The judge advanced further into the room, the stillness of which was so profound that the detective could hear the ticking of his own watch.

'Have the necessary arrangements been made outside?' asked Mr. Mallin, and Mrs. Evans nodded.

'Excellent,' went on the judge. 'Excellent. How nice it is to be able to depend on one's friends. I daresay you appreciate that, Mr. Blackmore? No doubt you have at times suffered from the inefficiency of subordinates?'

'Suppose we cut the preliminaries,' said the detective curtly. 'All this fine talk may be very nice for Mr. Justice Mallin, a judge on the King's Bench, but it's a little incongruous coming from the brother of a murderer — a man who was hanged!'

A spasm of rage distorted the other's face, and he glared his hatred with eyes that were scarcely sane.

'My brother was the greatest man who ever lived,' he cried harshly. 'A genius! Do not dare to malign his memory with your foul lips! But for you he would be living to-day!'

'It was you who sentenced him to death!' retorted Blackmore, and the judge reeled as though he had been struck.

'I have never forgotten it,' he said hoarsely. 'I could not get out of it without arousing suspicion, and the compact among all of us was that we would none of us do anything that would arouse suspicion against the others. That is why

Simon lived alone instead of with his wife. He was prepared, should misfortune overtake him, to suffer alone and in silence, and no one could point to his family with a finger of scorn. He was a great man, a wonderful man, although he admitted that I possessed more organising genius than he. I planned all his operations!'

'You have been wonderful, James,' said the woman, and Mr. Justice Mallin bowed.

'I have tried to be worthy of my brother,' he said simply, and a suspicion that had been forming in Blackmore's brain became a certainty.

The judge was mad!

Not outwardly. Not by any form of eccentricity that would mark him out from his sane fellow men, but undoubtedly mad for all that. His mania was unnoticeable and seemed to lie only in the abnormal hero-worship that he extended to the dead forger.

'That day, when by force of circumstances, I was forced to send my brother to an ignoble death,' continued Mr.

Justice Mallin, 'I swore that I would punish every one that was connected with his downfall. I have kept my word. You, very luckily, played into my hands the day you called to see me at Hillbrow. The many attempts that had been made on your life had failed, and I was getting anxious. That letter was written especially for your benefit, and also to avoid anyone suspecting me. Had you not called to see me that morning I should have got into communication with you, using that letter as an excuse, and persuaded you to do what you eventually did — stay with me.

'If it had not been for your secretary my task would have been completed when I dropped the noose over your head from the roof. But no matter, it was only delayed. To-night we shall settle accounts.'

'Was it you who killed Jellis?' asked the detective.

Mr. Mallin inclined his head.

'Yes,' he answered. 'It was I who also killed James Lane. I wrote to Fletcher asking him to come and see me at Hillbrow as I had something to tell him which could be to his advantage. I told him to say nothing to anybody and to bring my letter with him. If he had not brought it or had told his wife where he was coming to I should have offered him a job and let him go. He did bring the letter and he had not told his wife!'

'And Jellis?' said Blackmore. 'How did you decoy him from Hanley?'

'Very simply,' said the judge. 'John — my other brother, whom I think you met on the night of Fletcher's death at Simon's house, wrote him a letter purporting to come from a firm of solicitors and stating that he had been left a legacy. It asked him to come up to London at once and stated the train he was to travel by. John met him at the station. The rest was easy. He was brought to the field where he met his death just after midnight, and I was waiting for him. For a man who had killed so many wretches he made a great fuss,' added Mr. Mallin reminiscently.

'Don't you think you are wasting a lot of time,' suggested the yellow-faced woman. 'It would be as well to finish — and go!'

'Yes, yes, you are quite right,' said Mr. Mallin, and began to fumble in the pocket of his coat.

'What are you going to do with his secretary?' asked the woman.

'With Cartwright?' The judge raised his eyebrows. 'Is he still unconscious?'

She nodded.

'Yes. He did recover but John gave him another shot of the drug.'

'Excellent!' Mr. Justice Mallin thought for a moment, then his brow cleared. 'He has been with Mr. Blackmore for many years,' he said. 'It would be a great pity to separate them in death! The grave I instructed Charles and John to dig in the back garden should be six feet deep. There will be room for them both, and as the young man is still unconscious there will be no need for me to trouble further with him. He can be placed on the top of his employer before they fill in the hole!'

'You fiend!' burst out John Blackmore as the other's meaning flashed to his mind. 'You're going to bury him alive!'

'He will not live long,' said the judge evenly, and took from his pocket the thing he had been fumbling for. It was a stout piece of rubber tubing about twelve inches long.

'You have probably been wondering how I intend that you should meet your end,' he went on, checking the angry flood that rose to the detective's lips. 'Possibly you have been considering the various methods such as stabbing, shooting, or something equally painless. Even you, my dear, in all probability pictured some such method?' He looked across at the woman for confirmation.

Her attitude was curious. She seemed entirely under the spell of the judge's personality. She was gazing at him and hanging on every word.

'I have, however,' he continued, 'thought the matter out, and I do not think that any of those methods are suitable for the man who brought Simon to his death. This,' he held up the piece of tubing, 'is weighted with shot. With it it is possible to beat a man so that he is beyond recognition! Beat him until he dies!'

'Great heavens!' The woman went deathly white at the horrible suggestion his words conveyed. Even she felt revolted.

'We will not waste any further time,' said Mr. Justice Mallin.

He took off his coat, laid it on the bare floor and began deliberately to roll up his sleeves.

'I — I — I think I'll go,' said Mrs. Evans, licking her bloodless lips.

'Perhaps it would be as well,' agreed Mr. Mallin. 'If you tell John and Charles to come in in ten minutes everything will be — er — ready for them.'

'All right,' she muttered and went out.

John Blackmore made a last desperate effort to free his hands as the judge stooped and picked up his terrible weapon, but it was useless. He was helpless, and at the mercy of a man who hated him with hatred that bordered on the fanatical.

'Now!' Mr. Justice Mallin dropped his pleasant tone, and his face was the face of a devil. 'The end is very near, Mr. John Blackmore! A fitting end! Every blow that I strike will be in payment for the hours of mental suffering that you caused my brother!'

He came close and raised the loaded tube, but the expected blow never fell.

There was a grinding of brakes, a rush of feet outside and a fusillade of shots.

Mr. Mallin swung round with a snarl that showed his yellow teeth, and the next second he was struggling furiously in the grasp of two big men who, accompanied by a third, had burst into the room.

'Thank Heavens — Kenton!' muttered John Blackmore huskily as he recognised the third man, and then his over-strained nerves gave way, and he fainted in the inspector's arms!

25

The Morning After

It was ten o'clock on the following morning and Kenton and John Blackmore were seated on the lawn at Hillbrow. That house and the Evans' and also Mr. Basil Stacey's bungalow were in the hands of the police.

Mrs. Evans and the man Charles had been taken to the local police station at Esher, whence Mr. Basil Stacey joined them when he arrived at the empty house on the arterial road.

'He never noticed that 'Lightning Sam' had pinched the letter the judge had written him explaining that they were going to decoy you to that place,' said Kenton. 'So when he arrived we were waiting for him. It's a good job that little 'dip' did sneak it, too, otherwise you wouldn't be here, Blackmore.'

The detective shivered.

The recollection of the time spent in that bare, white-washed room was an unpleasant memory.

'What was the idea with regard to Fryman?' he enquired. 'Have you found out?'

'I've found out everything,' replied the Scotland Yard man with satisfaction. 'Charles Evans has given the whole show away. He caved in completely when he knew the game was up. Simon Boyle, or, to give him his right name, David Mallin, had three brothers, Charles, Edward James, and John, who was as like him as two peas in a pod. They weren't twins but they took after the mother. James and Charles were like the father.'

'I noticed the likeness the night Charles dined here,' said Blackmore. 'But it only struck me as a coincidence.'

Kenton nodded.

'Well,' he continued, 'the three brothers seemed to be pretty well tarred with the same brush. They were all criminals at heart — out after easy money. James planned all the coups and David, who was a genius with his pen, carried them out. The others did more or less as they were told. Quite early they all decided to take different names, and lead separate lives, which they carried out. The reason was that they knew that if they kept together and one of them was detected the disgrace would fall upon every member of the family, besides which, if they weren't connected in any way there was more chance of the others helping.

'Then David met a girl, the daughter of a crook financier called Evans, and married her. The result of the marriage was Basil. Charles also married but his wife died in giving birth to a girl. The one who took the most risk was David and he insisted that his wife passed herself off as the wife of his brother Charles, and that the girl Sonia, Charles' daughter, should appear to be her child. Their own boy was sent to school in the name of Stacey, and retained this name when he came of age and joined the gang — if you can call a family affair by that name.

'It was a novel scheme, and it worked.

'Either Basil or Sonia or Charles Evans were always on the spot to act as 'cover' when David operated, and it was their job to carry the gun and contrive to pass it to him in an emergency, as Stacey did at Colchester.

'James' hobby was law, and he worked his way up until he became a judge, and it was he who got hold of the people's signatures that David forged, and saw that the legal documents were properly drawn up.

'I'm telling you what I got out of Charles last night. I couldn't get a word out of the woman, or John and Stacey, and the shock has sent Mallin completely batty. He's nothing more or less than a raving lunatic. I should think he was always on the borderline.'

'I came to that conclusion last night,' said Blackmore gravely. 'But you haven't told me what they were going to do with Fryman. Why did they want his wallet?'

Kenton took out a cigar case and extracted an evil looking weed. Blackmore hastily offered him one of his own and the inspector accepted with evident gratification.

'Well,' he said, when it was alight. 'It

seems that there wasn't so much money in the safe at Boyle's place — I must call him Boyle, I've always thought of him in that name — as they had anticipated. He held the reserve fund and he must have been dipping into it pretty freely. Anyway, finances were low and they had to hit upon some means of replenishing the exchequer.

'It was David who suggested the idea before his death. Sonia was pretty friendly with Fryman, had met him at a dance, and had been with him to theatres and things. There was nothing in it on either side, they were just friendly, but everyone knew of the friendship and had seen 'em out a lot together.

'David's idea was this. To get hold of Fryman's signature and make a will leaving his fortune to Sonia. Fryman used to carry his name and address written on a card in his wallet. And it was an excellent specimen of his usual signature. Sonia had happened to mention this to David, and that probably started the scheme. Anyway, he had to get a specimen of the millionaire's signature, and that was the job that Stacey offered 'Harry the Dip.'

'Well, you know what happened to Harry. He got suspicious. Stacey said more than he ought, and Harry followed him and discovered the identity of Simon Boyle. He got into Boyle's house and heard them planning the Colchester coup. He was probably thinking of blackmail first, and then he thought it would be safer to give Boyle away and cotton the reward. But to get on:

'When they found that money was scarce, James, who was able to copy a signature nearly as well as David, decided to go through with this plan. So Stacey got hold of 'Lightning Sam', and that really was their undoing. Pleasant family, aren't they?'

Kenton blew a cloud of smoke into the golden sunlight.

'And after the will had been drawn up?' said Blackmore.

The Scotland Yard man shrugged his shoulders.

'It would have spelt the doom of Mr. Fryman,' he said soberly.

'Was the girl in the plot?' asked Blackmore.

Kenton shook his head.

'No, they dare not tell her,' he replied. 'She was the only one they weren't sure of. By the way, she never went to a nursing home. That was all my eye. She never left the Evans' house. John came disguised as a doctor for the benefit of the men who were watching, and a dummy was driven out in a car. They locked her in a top room, even the servants didn't know. We let her out this morning.'

Blackmore looked over to a secluded part of the grounds where two figures were just visible, in earnest conversation.

'She hasn't been long in getting into communication with her friends,' he murmured, and smiled.

'Who's with her?' grunted Kenton.

'Young Morris,' answered the detective. 'He is quite a decent sort, and so is the girl. She tried to do her best for me although she very naturally hated me.'

Kenton rose and threw away his cigar.

'Well, good luck to 'em,' he remarked. 'She must have had a pretty rotten time in that atmosphere from a kid upwards. It'll do her good to get out of it. I'm going down to the station, Blackmore, to arrange about having those beauties transferred to London, are you coming with me?'

John Blackmore nodded and together they strolled across the lawn.

★ ★ ★

Mrs. Evans never stood her trial. In the heel of her shoe she had concealed a small quantity of poison in preparation for such an emergency as had overtaken her, and she was found stretched out on the floor of her cell, her lined yellow face smooth and youthful in death.

Mr. Justice Mallin, hopelessly insane, was sent to Broadmoor for the rest of his natural life, and both Charles and John Mallin received life sentences. Basil Stacey got off with ten years, and was taken from the dock vowing vengeance against all and sundry when he got out.

'He'll cool down after the first five years,' said Kenton as he took leave of

Blackmore on the steps of the Old Bailey. 'Nothing like Dartmoor as a sedative! By the way, I haven't seen anything of the girl Sonia throughout the trial.'

'You wouldn't be likely to,' said John Blackmore. 'She's in France with Harry Morris.'

'What, married?' exclaimed the inspector, in surprise.

'I sincerely hope so,' retorted Blackmore. 'Really, my dear Kenton, you shouldn't say such things before my young secretary!' and Cartwright grinned at the Scotland Yard man's genuine embarrassment.

THE END

We do hope that you have enjoyed reading this large print book.

Did you know that all of our titles are available for purchase?

We publish a wide range of high quality large print books including:
Romances, Mysteries, Classics
General Fiction
Non Fiction and Westerns

Special interest titles available in large print are:
The Little Oxford Dictionary
Music Book, Song Book
Hymn Book, Service Book

Also available from us courtesy of Oxford University Press:
Young Readers' Dictionary
(large print edition)
Young Readers' Thesaurus
(large print edition)

For further information or a free brochure, please contact us at:
Ulverscroft Large Print Books Ltd.,
The Green, Bradgate Road, Anstey,
Leicester, LE7 7FU, England.
Tel: (00 44) **0116 236 4325**
Fax: (00 44) **0116 234 0205**

Other titles in the
Linford Mystery Library:

DEATH ASKS THE QUESTION

John Russell Fearn

Seemingly grand from the outside, the interior of Abner Hilton's house was a dilapidated, gloomy place — reflecting its morbid and desperately impoverished occupant. But Hilton's insane plan would lift him out of his poverty. He would murder his young niece, who was about to visit him; her dead father's will would ensure that her considerable wealth would pass to him. However, when his plan was put into operation, the young woman's horrifying death was to have terrifying repercussions . . .

ENTER JIMMY STRANGE

Ernest Dudley

'What type of skulduggery is the Master Mind contemplating this time?' That was the question put to Jimmy Strange by his long-suffering girlfriend Sandra. But the answer always depended on which type of criminals Jimmy was pitting his wits against. Whether they were poisoners, gunmen, murderers, drug dealers, or jewel thieves, they were all operating, untouched, outside the law — until Jimmy entered the scene — and he was not averse to using their own methods against them . . .

THE VEILS OF DEATH

Nigel Vane

In the same house that his father had committed suicide, Dick Lamont is found brutally stabbed and dying. The last words he utters are odd: 'Caught me . . . never guessed . . . the seventh . . . ' Lamont's sister tells the investigating detective that, just before he died, their father had entrusted her with two silken squares, embroidered with strange black lines; their purpose unknown. Was there any connection between them and the murder in the empty house?

THE LAST WARNING

Gerald Verner

Detective-Superintendent Budd is a busy man. In Thatchford on a minor investigation, calling on his old friend Superintendent Hawkins, he's asked to help with a murder mystery. One man has been stabbed, two of his business associates have been threatened. Then another murder takes place in a locked room with police guards outside . . . The case bristles with difficulties, but Budd sifts all the clues with his usual thoroughness, and exposes a dastardly plot.

NO GOLD FOR TINA

John Robb

Newspaper reporter Desmond Tearle, investigating the murder of racketeer Daks Hale, finds that the principal suspect has been framed. Then he discovers that Hale's mistress, the deadly Tina Tallan, had arranged the murder and intends to take over Hale's gang. Tearle, the object of her desire, becomes embroiled in Tina's world, as he assists her in a bank robbery. And when the robbery goes wrong, the bodies begin to pile up, with Tearle himself earmarked for a cruel death . . .

A CASE FOR BRUTUS LLOYD

John Russell Fearn

Dr. Brutus Lloyd was no more than four feet ten inches tall, an amazingly gnome-like man. The most surprising thing about him was his deep bass voice. A brilliant scientist and criminologist, his unorthodox methods caused consternation to Inspector Branson of the New York City Police when: an accident caused a mining engineer to see into 'another world'; four scientists were murdered for their collective brainpower, and when dinosaurs were seen on the outskirts of a village . . .